out of time

Other books in the Time Thriller Trilogy:

Ripple Effect (Book One)

time thriller trilogy

out of time

paul mccusker

ZONDERVAN®

ZONDERVAN.com/
AUTHORTRACKER
follow your favorite authors

Out of Time
Copyright © 2009 by Paul McCusker

Requests for information should be addressed to:
Zondervan, Grand Rapids, Michigan 49530

Library of Congress Cataloging-in-Publication Data

McCusker, Paul, 1958-
    Out of time / Paul McCusker.
        p. cm. — (Time thriller trilogy ; bk. 2)
        Summary: A man on horseback wearing medieval garments and claiming to be King Arthur arrives in Fawlt Line, Maryland, teenaged Elizabeth's hometown that may be a portal to alternate times and unexpected time travels.
        ISBN 978-0-310-71437-8 (softcover)
        [1. Space and time — Fiction. 2. Time travel — Fiction. 3. Arthur, King — Fiction. 4. Christian life — Fiction.] I. Title.
PZ7.M47841635Ou 2009
[Fic] — dc22

                                                                              2008044638

Published in association with the literary agency of Alive Communications, Inc., 7680 Goddard Street, Suite 200, Colorado Springs, CO 80920. www.alivecommunications.com

Interior design by Christine Orejuela-Winkelman

Printed in the United States of America

09 10 11 12 13 14 • 24 23 22 21 20 19 18 17 16 15 14 13 12 11 10 9 8 7 6 5 4 3 2 1

With deepest appreciation to the many authors who helped fill in the pieces with their works: Geoffrey Ashe, Henry Gilbert and his *King Arthur's Knights*, Sidney Lanier with *The Boy's King Arthur*, Ronan Coghlan with *The Encyclopedia of Arthurian Legends*, and Kenneth McLeish's *Myths and Folk Stories of Britain and Ireland*. I'm also grateful to the staff members of the British Embassy in Washington, D.C., the British Consulate in Denver, Philip Glassborow, Ruth and Gareth Mayers and, mostly, my wife, Elizabeth, who shared the joy of that first image of King Arthur being knocked off of a horse on the motorway.

"Quid est ergo tempus? si nemo ex me quaerat, scio; si quaerenti explicare velim, nescio."

[Translation: "What, then, is time? If no one asks me, I know; if I want to explain it to someone who does ask me, I do not know."]

–St. Augustine

Prologue

On the pinnacle of Glastonbury Tor, an unusual cone-like hill with a tower named after a saint, a tall, old man stood in the wet English twilight. The wind whipped his long gray hair and beard, and the ragged brown monk's robe he wore trembled like a flag in a gale. The dark clouds above moved and gathered around him. Chalice and Wearyall Hills sat nearby, their shoulders hunched. A battered Abbey beyond listened in silence.

The man cast a sad eye to the green landscape, spread like a quilt, adorned with small houses and shops. He prayed silently for a moment, then pulled an ancient curved horn from under his habit. He placed it to his lips and blew once, then twice, then a final time. The three muted blasts were caught by the wind and carried away.

It was a summons.

I

The Stranger

I II III IV V VI VII VIII IX X XI XII

"This is a beautiful flower," Elizabeth Forde said to her boyfriend, Jeff. She lifted the small white corsage and breathed deeply. "It's amazing."

They were in Jeff's old Volkswagen Bug, heading for the Fawlt Line High School end-of-the-year school dance.

You're amazing, Jeff wanted to say, but blushed instead as he looked her over for the umpteenth time. She was wearing a stunning pink gown with the white corsage he had bought for her pinned to the strap. She smiled at him and he wished he had a camera to catch her in that moment: her delicate nose, large brown eyes and full lips, all framed by the long brown hair that she'd taken extra care with earlier that evening. She was beautiful.

"What?" she asked self-consciously.

"Nothing," he said, blushing again and tugging at the collar of his ill-fitting formal shirt. He turned his attention to the road, which had strangely disappeared. "Whoa!" he shouted.

They had driven into a thick wall of fog. The open fields on both sides of the road were suddenly gone and the road itself was reduced to a sound beneath their tires. Jeff slowed down and, though the sun was setting somewhere beyond their visibility, he turned on the headlights. The beams seemed to hit the grainy whiteness of the fog and bounce back.

Elizabeth gasped. "Where did this come from?"

"I better pull over," Jeff said — and did, the gravel crunching under their tires as he came to a stop. He left the engine running and the headlights shining into the thick white soup. "Let's wait for a few minutes to see if it lifts."

Elizabeth hugged herself and shivered. "This is creepy. I've never seen fog like this around Fawlt Line. At least not this early in the evening."

"It's strange. But we're in safe territory." Jeff pointed just to their right. The fog seemed to spin and swirl around a sign attached to a chain-link fence only a few feet away. *Coming Soon: The Dubbs' Historical Village*, the sign proclaimed.

Malcolm Dubbs was the wealthiest citizen of the little town of Fawlt Line, the next-to-last member of a family that had been in the area for close to two centuries. Malcolm, a member of the English branch of the Dubbs family, came to America to be the custodian of the Dubbs' vast estate after a tragic accident took the lives of his American cousin Thomas Dubbs and his wife. That also left Malcolm to serve as the guardian of their surviving teenage son, Jeff.

"I never thought he'd get away with it," Elizabeth said, referring to the Historical Village.

Jeff looked ahead at the fog. It reminded him of a movie screen right before a film is about to start. "He's had his share of battles over it."

It was well-known that Malcolm Dubbs had been determined to create this village the moment he moved to America two years before.

"You know that most of the people in town think he's insane," said Elizabeth.

Jeff smiled. "Sometimes I wonder myself."

"I heard them at the diner the other day." She put on an accent that sounded uncannily like old Ben Hearn. "Ya know what he's doin' with that there Village, right? He's shippin' in *buildings*,

I'm tellin' ya. Brick by brick and stone by stone from all over the cotton-pickin' world. Have ya ever heard of such a thing? A museum with a few trinkets and artifacts I can understand, but *buildings*?'"

Jeff began to laugh.

Elizabeth continued her imitation of Old Ben. "Do ya know what they been workin' on over the past few weeks? Some kind of a *ruin* from England. A *ruin*! A monastery or castle or cathedral or somethin'. Why wouldn't he buy somethin' *new*? We got plenty of old stuff around here already."

Elizabeth was laughing with Jeff now.

"It must have cost him a lot of money to ship in this fog too," Jeff added.

They continued to laugh until they heard a high, shrill sound from somewhere outside.

"What was that?" Elizabeth asked, quickly becoming serious and looking around.

"I don't know." Jeff peered into the fog. "Some kind of animal."

The sound came again. This time it was closer and recognizable: the high, agitated whinny of a horse.

"Who'd be horseback riding at this time?" Jeff asked. "And in this fog?"

"I think we should go," Elizabeth said, her voice rising. She was holding tightly onto the dashboard, her knuckles white.

"Bits," Jeff said. "It's only a — "

"I've got this feeling," Elizabeth whispered. Her eyes were wide, panicked. "It reminds me of that feeling I had before."

"Before?"

"Please, Jeff — just go."

"Okay." Jeff put the car in gear and carefully guided the car back onto the tarmac. He hoped that the fog might lift or, of greater importance, that the horse wasn't on the road ahead.

"Does Malcolm have horses for the Village?" Elizabeth asked, making conversation as if to calm herself.

"Yes, but the stables are on the other side of our land."

"Maybe one got out."

"Maybe." Jeff began fumbling in his jacket pocket. "Take my cell phone and call him."

Elizabeth reached over to take the phone. Jeff glanced at her, then back to the road just in time to see a large shadow take form in front of them. As they bore down on it, a horse — *the* horse — frightened by the sudden appearance of the car, reared wildly up on its hind legs, screaming at them.

"Hold on!" Jeff shouted, jerking the steering wheel to the right as he hit the brakes with full force. The Volkswagen skidded to a stop only a few feet from the horse, which came down on all fours and then reared onto its hind legs again. This time Elizabeth and Jeff heard a shout, and a figure on the horse's back fell onto the ground.

Jeff and Elizabeth looked at each other, shaking.

"Did you hit them?" Elizabeth asked.

"No." Jeff pushed his door open. "Stay here," he said before the door slammed itself shut. He opened it again and reached in to turn on the emergency flashers. "Find the cell phone. I think it fell on the floor when we stopped."

"Be careful!" she shouted after him.

Jeff made his way cautiously toward the horse, which snorted at him and then dashed away into the fog. "Hello? Are you all right?" Jeff called out.

The fog seemed to part like a curtain, as if to present the figure lying on the road like an actor on a stage.

"Oh no," Jeff said, rushing forward. He crouched down next to the figure, a very large man. Whoever it was seemed to be wrapped in a dark blanket. The man was perfectly still and his face was hidden in the shadows.

"Hey," Jeff said, hoping the man would stir. He didn't. Jeff looked him over for any sign of blood. Nothing was obvious around his head. But what could he expect to see in that fog? He turned toward his car and shouted, "Elizabeth! Call nine-one-one on the cell phone. And bring me the flashlight from the glove compartment!"

He peered closely at the shadowed form of the man as he heard Elizabeth open her door. She was already talking into the phone, giving instructions frantically to an emergency operator. The shaft of light from the flashlight bounced around eerily in the ever-moving fog.

"Jeff?"

"Here," Jeff said.

Elizabeth joined him. "Ambulance is on its way. But they're on the line and want to know his condition."

He took the flashlight from her and got his first full look at the stranger. He had long, dark salt-and-peppery hair, a beard and moustache, and a rugged, lined face. Jeff couldn't guess an age for the man. Anywhere from forty to sixty, he figured. The man wore a peaceful expression and could've been sleeping. Finally, Jeff responded, "I can't tell. There's no blood."

Elizabeth reported Jeff's findings to the emergency operator, then asked Jeff, "He's not dead, is he?"

"I don't think so." Jeff reached down, separating the blanket to check the man's vital signs. The feel of the cloth told him it wasn't a blanket at all. And as he pushed the fabric aside, he realized that it was a cape made of a thick, course material, clasped at the neck by a dragon brooch. "What in the world — ?"

Elizabeth gasped.

They expected to see a shirt or a sweater or a coat of some sort. Instead he wore a long vest with the symbol of a dragon stitched onto the front, a gold belt, brown leggings, and soft leather footwear that looked more like slippers than shoes. The whole outfit reminded Jeff of the kind of costume he'd seen in a Robin Hood movie. At his side was a sword in a sheath.

"Is it Halloween?" Elizabeth asked.

15

◌ ◌ ◌

At the high school, the dance was just getting under way. Dry Heaves, a rock band from nearby Hancock, warmed up for their first number as the sound engineer tried to get the volume just right.

Malcolm Dubbs, dressed in a tux and looking all the more dashing for it, stepped into the converted gymnasium and winced at the cacophony of heavy drums and rapid-fire lyrics coming from the stage. *I'm getting old*, he thought. A handful of students mingled in the middle of the dance floor and along the walls. Streamers and balloons blew gently in the rafters above. A banner wishing the students a good summer rustled over the scoreboard.

What was I thinking? he wondered. *What possessed me to allow Jeff and Elizabeth to talk me into chaperoning this dance?*

A tap on the shoulder took his gaze from the dance floor and into the round face of Sheriff Richard Hounslow. The sheriff was in his uniform — Fawlt Line Police Department's traditional beige shirt and trousers. His only official equipment was his badge and a walkie-talkie strapped to his belt; he never wore a gun unless he had to. "I need to talk to you," Hounslow mouthed over the music and hooked a thumb toward the door.

Malcolm nodded and followed him out. They walked down the passageway until the music was just a throbbing bump on the other side of the walls.

"What can I do for you, Sheriff?" Malcolm asked. He braced himself, not for bad news, but for trouble. Hounslow was fairly open with his dislike for Malcolm. Why the sheriff didn't like him, however, was something Malcolm couldn't figure out.

Hounslow hitched his thumbs in his belt and looked at Malcolm from head to toe. "You're a regular James Bond, aren't you? Put a woman on each elbow, sit you at a gaming table, and you're good to go. Go on, say the words."

"Words?"

"The name's Bond, James Bond."

"Honestly, Sheriff — "

"You've got the accent for it. Go ahead."

Malcolm sighed. "Is there a *legitimate* reason you asked me to leave the dance? They were playing my favorite song, you know."

Hounslow raised an eyebrow. "Have you checked your cell phone lately?"

Malcolm looked puzzled and took the small phone out of his jacket pocket. It was on — but with all the noise, he hadn't heard it ring. The message symbol flashed, and the screen indicated that he'd missed several calls from Jeff. He looked at Hounslow with alarm.

"Jeff and Elizabeth are okay, but you need to come to the hospital. Apparently they had a near miss with one of the workers from your so-called historical village."

"What kind of near miss?"

"Apparently the man came racing off of your property on a horse — right in front of Jeff. Worse, he doesn't speak a word of English, just some gibberish. That's why I need you to come." The two men started walking down the school hallway toward the parking lot.

"Was anyone hurt?" Malcolm asked, still concerned.

"No. But Doc McConnell wants to keep him overnight for observation."

"I can't imagine how the man could be one of my workers," Malcolm said, surprised. "They're off for the weekend. Are you certain he's from my village?"

"He has to be. No one else would wear an outfit like he had on."

Malcolm turned to the sheriff with a quizzical expression.

"You'll see," the sheriff said.

"Are you two all right?" Malcolm asked Jeff and Elizabeth as he approached the hospital room.

"A little shaken — but okay," Jeff said.

Malcolm paused to look at Elizabeth in her formal gown. "You look lovely."

"Thank you," she said with a slight blush and a smile.

"You don't have to stay here," Malcolm said. "Go to the dance. I'll take care of things now."

Jeff and Elizabeth glanced at one another, and then Jeff spoke. "Not a chance. We want to find out who this guy is and what he was doing."

"And why he was wearing those strange clothes," Elizabeth added.

Malcolm nodded. He would have reacted the same way.

"In here," Sheriff Hounslow said.

Malcolm followed him into the room, which was lit up by fluorescent lights overhead.

"He had caused such a ruckus when they brought him in — shouting, trying to get away — that the doctor had to sedate him and strap him to the bed," Hounslow explained.

The room was basic, with the bed, various monitors, a small end table, and institutional wooden closet. Dr. McConnell stood next to one of the monitors, checking the numbers on a clipboard.

"We had to give him three times the normal dose because of his size," Dr. McConnell said softly, as if he was afraid of waking the man.

Malcolm looked closely at the unconscious figure. He was big, all right, stretching the length of the bed. "I've never seen him before," Malcolm said.

"He was riding one of our horses," Jeff stated. "Bullet — the black stallion."

Malcolm cocked an eyebrow. "I'll have to talk to Mr. Farrar, my groundskeeper. He lives in the cottage next to the stables."

"Already done," Hounslow said. "He was watching television. Didn't hear a thing. He was surprised that one of your horses was gone. So, if nothing else, you could press charges against the man for horse-thievery."

Malcolm shook his head. "I'd like to find out more about him first."

"Well, good luck. We couldn't get anything out of him. He kept yakking away in some gibberish and was pounding his chest and calling himself Rex or Regis or something like that."

"King'?" Malcolm asked. "Rex — or Regis — is Latin for *king*."

"I told you," Elizabeth said with a jab at Jeff.

"I didn't say you were wrong," Jeff replied defensively.

Dr. McConnell said, "The words and phrases certainly reminded me of some of the Latin I picked up in medical school."

"He was speaking Latin in entire sentences?" Malcolm asked.

"I suppose so," Dr. McConnell said. "But I'm no expert."

Hounslow pulled at his belt. "I called the mental hospital in Grantsville to see if they've had any escapes. None."

"Just because he speaks Latin doesn't mean he's mentally disturbed," Elizabeth said. "My dad speaks Latin."

Hounslow looked as if he might say something unkind, but decided against it. Instead, he said, "Fine, but what about *this*?" He went to the closet and opened the door. The stranger's clothes were hung inside on different hangers.

Malcolm walked to the closet and looked at the robe, the tunic, the leggings, the cape, and the belt. "This is what he had on?" he asked, surprised.

Hounslow nodded. "That's another reason we figured he was from your village."

"I told him we haven't started hiring character actors yet," Jeff said.

"The construction workers are still building," Malcolm said. "I haven't hired any of the staff yet." He fingered the fabric of the

19

robe and tunic, making a mental note of the dragon insignias. He picked up the soft leather shoes and looked them over. "Amazing. The outfit looks so authentic. And I don't mean authentic like a well-done replica, I mean it looks *worn,* like they're his real clothes."

"Maybe he's one of those homeless fruitcakes who just happened to wander into town," Hounslow offered.

Dr. McConnell folded his arms. "It's hard to imagine this guy being homeless and just wandering anywhere with that sword."

"Sword?" asked Malcolm.

"Here," Hounslow said and reached farther into the closet. With both hands he pulled out a long sword encased in an ornate golden scabbard. He cradled it in his arms for Malcolm to inspect.

"Good heavens," Malcolm gasped, running his hand along the scabbard. "Is that real gold?"

"Looks like it," Hounslow said.

Malcolm examined the handle of the sword, also golden, which had a row of unfamiliar jewels imbedded along the length of the stem. Even in the washed-out fluorescent light of the room, it sparkled as if it reflected the sun. "May I take it out?"

"Yeah," Hounslow said, "but be careful. It's heavy and *sharp.*"

Malcolm grabbed the handle with both hands and withdrew the sword from the scabbard. It was heavy, as Hounslow said, and Malcolm imagined it would take a man the size of the stranger to wield it with any effect. It was even a strain to hold it up. The blade was made of thick, shiny steel with an elaborate engraving along the edges of what looked like thin vines and blossoms. "It must be worth a fortune," Malcolm said as he slid the sword back into the sheath.

Dr. McConnell agreed. "So what's a derelict doing with a Latin vocabulary and a valuable sword?"

"That's what I'd like to find out when he wakes up," Malcolm answered.

2

I II III IV V VI VII VIII IX X XI XII

Within two hours the stranger was awake and pulling at the restraining straps on the bed. He shouted at the nurse, Dr. McConnell, Sheriff Hounslow, Jeff, Elizabeth, and Malcolm in a tone that was unmistakably belligerent. When he realized it didn't help, he resigned himself to watching the flashing lights and electronic graphs on the medical equipment around him.

After hearing a few of the phrases he yelled — like *rex, regis, libertas, stultus* — Malcolm was certain about the language. "I studied a bit of Latin when I was at Oxford. But that was a long time ago and I've put it out of my mind since," he lamented. "Let me ring a friend of mine from the University at Frostburg."

Dr. Camilla Ashe was so intrigued by Malcolm's description that she drove the forty-five minutes to Fawlt Line that night, arriving at the hospital a little after eleven. By that time the group in the room included Jerry Anderson, editor of Fawlt Line's *Daily Gazette*. He had heard the news about the mystery man on his police scanner. Hounslow stood silently against the wall, his arms folded and a scowl stuck on his face. Jeff and Elizabeth sat against the opposite wall and tried to stay out of the way.

Dr. Ashe, a prim, scholarly woman dressed from head to toe in tweed, approached the side of the bed. The stranger was once again transfixed by the lights on the equipment and didn't seem to realize she was there until she cleared her throat. He looked at her with an expression of impatience, and when she spoke to him in Latin he gawked at her. Then, realizing he finally had someone who understood him, he bombarded her with words. She tried to interject, but the stranger kept talking. His voice eventually rose to a shout and Dr. Ashe seemed to lose patience with him. She shouted back with as much force as she could muster, speaking in a tone that was withering in any language. The stranger finally turned his head away from her as if to say that the conversation was over and didn't look at her again. She spun around to the expectant group, growled loudly, and stormed out of the room.

"What was that all about?" Malcolm asked her in the hall.

Her hands trembled as she unwrapped a piece of gum and tossed it into her mouth. "I'd love to have a cigarette right now."

"But you don't smoke," Malcolm said.

"I'm willing to start."

"What in the world were you saying?" Hounslow asked as he too entered the hallway. "I thought I might have to separate you two."

She took a deep breath, as if her indignation could hardly be controlled. "He said he didn't want to talk to a woman. He said he resented a woman being sent to him by his captors."

"Captors!"

Dr. Ashe shook her head forcefully. "I don't mind saying that this man should be certified. He's not sane."

"Why? What did he say?"

"He said that, as a king, he should be treated with more respect. He wants to speak with whichever Baron or Duke is holding him captive. He wants to know where he's being held and if there's a ransom. He demands to be told how he got here and where his knights are. And, finally, he wants someone to tell him about the magic boxes with the flashing lights." Dr. Ashe groaned.

"I told you he's a fruitcake," Sheriff Hounslow said to Malcolm.

"Or it's a very tiresome joke," Dr. Ashe added and wagged a finger at Malcolm. "You wouldn't be pulling a prank on me, would you?"

"Not at all," Malcolm said simply.

"Then you should get him some psychiatric help," she said.

"I still don't understand," Malcolm said. "He said he's a king. But King *who* — and king of *what*?"

Dr. Ashe frowned. "He says he's *King Arthur*."

3

I II III IV V VI VII VIII IX X XI XII

Dr. Ashe left. She wanted nothing more to do with the Latin-speaking lunatic.

"What are you going to do now?" Jerry Anderson asked Malcolm.

Before Malcolm could answer, Hounslow jumped in. "Let's get something straight. Doc McConnell and I are making the decisions here. Not Malcolm."

"Sorry," Jerry said. "What are you going to do now, Sheriff Hounslow?"

Hounslow shrugged. "I don't know yet."

Malcolm smiled politely. "In my humble opinion, we should find someone else who knows enough Latin to communicate with him. A man this time."

Elizabeth raised her hand and wiggled her fingers. "I know someone."

All eyes fell to her.

My dad," she said. "Like I said before, he speaks Latin. He studied it when he was in college and sometimes uses it for his research." Elizabeth's father was a teacher at the middle school who often hired himself out as a researcher for other academics and authors. Some said with his obvious intelligence he should be teaching at a major university instead.

"Of course," Malcolm said and went to the phone.

Alan Forde was quite tall himself and his size, combined with his knowledge of Latin, obviously impressed the stranger. The stranger seemed more patient and spoke in calmer tones. Alan pulled up a chair next to the bed. After a brief conversation, he turned to Dr. McConnell. "Can we free his hands please?"

Dr. McConnell looked skeptically at Alan and the stranger. "You're kidding."

"He promises not to resort to physical violence or even to attempt an escape. But it's offensive to his honor to be tied up."

"Well . . ." Dr. McConnell began, then looked to Sheriff Hounslow and Malcolm for help.

"I think you should do it," Malcolm suggested.

Sheriff Hounslow unclipped the walkie-talkie from his belt and called to one of his officers on the other end. "Bring me my gun," he said.

Dr. McConnell began undoing the restraining straps. "Here goes," he said softly.

The stranger rubbed his wrists then sat up in the bed. He spoke to Alan.

"Thank you," Alan translated, then added, "I think he'll be more agreeable to talk now."

"Does he really think he's King Arthur?" Hounslow asked.

"Yes."

"Then what's he doing here?" Malcolm asked. "What was he doing on my property? Why did he take my horse?"

Alan posed the questions to the stranger.

Through Alan, the stranger explained, "My nephew Sir Mordred, that traitorous and wicked knight, attempted to usurp my throne whilst I was pursuing Sir Lancelot north to his castle at Joyous Gard. Verily, I loved Lancelot as my own, even whilst he coveted my queen and betrayed me. Whilst I was gone, Mordred enticed many weak-willed nobles to join his army to overthrow my rule. My army met and routed his forces on Barham Down, but my nephew fled to other parts. We made chase but did not battle them again, choosing instead to negotiate a peace. I desired not the terrible bloodshed that would ensue if we were to engage in combat. And so it is that we have come here to this plain to meet and discuss terms."

"What's this got to do with anything?" Hounslow growled.

Malcolm ignored him. "So tonight is the eve of your meeting with Mordred to make a truce," he said to Alan while looking at the stranger. "What happened?"

The stranger answered through Alan, "As I lay upon my bed in my pavilion, I dreamed an incredible dream. I sat upon a chair which was fastened to a wheel in the sky. I was adorned in a garment of finest woven gold. Far below me I saw deep black water wherein was contained all manner of serpents and worms and the most foul and horrible wild beasts. Suddenly, it was as if the wheel turned upside-down and I fell among the serpents and wild beasts and they pounced upon me. I cried out in a loud voice and awoke upon a cold slab of stone in the midst of a vast field. Troubled by this vision, I rose, determined to find my knights. I espied glowing torches in the distance and approached them. I found there not my army but a stable of horses. I mounted one and made haste in the direction of my knights. I spurred the horse ever faster and faster until I was attacked by the armored cart that was drawn by neither man nor beast. Frightened, my horse reared and I fell to the ground." He turned to Malcolm. "Now, speak, knave; am I a prisoner or is this a dream?"

Malcolm tugged gently at his ear and said to the others, "He woke up on one of the stone slabs in my historical village. Probably in the church ruins I bought from England. Very interesting."

"You don't believe any of this nonsense, do you?" Hounslow asked.

Malcolm answered in a guarded tone. "For the moment, I believe that he's confused and found himself on my property."

The stranger folded his arms and muttered the same phrase over and over.

"He says Merlin is responsible," Alan said. "He doesn't know how, but he's sure it is some trickery of Merlin's."

"That's it," Hounslow said. "Everybody out. It's now past midnight and I've had enough of this. We're going to transfer this nutcase to the Hancock mental hospital. Let *them* decide what to do with him." With that said, he marched out of the room.

Dr. McConnell looked at Malcolm apologetically. "What else can I do with him?"

Malcolm didn't know. "I wish I could take him back to my cottage."

The stranger spoke again and Alan translated, "Answer me! Am I to be ransomed or is this a dream?"

Malcolm spoke as soothingly as he could. "Tell him that we are not his captors and, if it'll help, to consider this a bizarre dream." As an afterthought, he added, "Also ask him if he'll give us his word as king not to try to escape tonight. Otherwise, the doctor will have to strap his arms again."

The stranger gave his word.

4

I II III IV V VI VII VIII IX X XI XII

The next morning Malcolm was at the breakfast table immersed in several books about the legends of King Arthur. Jeff dropped the *Fawlt Line Daily Gazette* in front of him. "Is He or Isn't He? Man Claims To Be King Arthur," the headline proclaimed in large type.

Malcolm glanced at it. "The front page, huh? I guess Jerry figured it was more exciting than the proposed resurfacing of Union Street."

"Malcolm," Jeff said, sitting in the chair opposite to him. "Do you really think he's King Arthur? I mean, I know better than anyone that weird things happen around here. But *King Arthur*? In Fawlt Line? Why?"

Malcolm gazed at his young nephew. "Beats me. That's why I'm refreshing myself on Arthurian legends. Maybe there's a clue in here somewhere."

"Unless he really *is* out of his mind."

"Of course," Malcolm said without conviction. "But if he's crazy, he knows his Arthur. Everything he described is in these books."

"Which part?"

"All of it. Mordred, who really was a nasty piece of work, tried to take over the kingdom while Arthur was out of the country chasing Lancelot. Arthur came back to fight him and they met on Salisbury Plain for a final battle." Malcolm turned the book on the table so Jeff could see it. He pointed to the facing page. "This is interesting. Some of the legends include the dream he told us about. Apparently it was so horrific he cried out and his knights came rushing in. He told them what he saw and his advisors said it was symbolic. Mordred would kill him in battle. They advised him to negotiate an agreement rather than fight. Arthur reluctantly agreed."

"Then what?"

"They met on the field to talk terms," Malcolm continued. "But the understanding was if any of the attending soldiers pulled out a weapon for any reason, then they'd battle. Legend has it that right as Arthur and Mordred came to an agreement about peace, a snake slithered over the foot of one of the knights. Arthur instinctively pulled out his sword to kill it. At the sight of the sword, Mordred cried out that it was a trick and instructed his men to attack. A slaughter followed."

"Who won?"

"Nobody."

Jeff frowned. "Nobody?"

"Mordred fatally wounded Arthur and Arthur killed Mordred. And that's where the legends split off into two different endings. One legend has Arthur dying and being buried somewhere. No one can agree where, though most say it was in a town called Glastonbury. Supposedly King Henry the Second found his body there during his reign."

"What's the other legend say?"

"That his body was taken away in a magical boat by the Lady of the Lake and her attendants."

Jeff smiled. "The Lady of the Lake."

Malcolm looked at Jeff impatiently. "The Lady who gave him the sword Excalibur. Don't you even know the *basics* of the story?"

"Nope."

Malcolm shoved the books at him. "Then your assignment for the day is to get familiar with it."

"But I'm out of school!" Jeff complained.

"We're *never* out of school, Jeff," Malcolm said.

Mrs. Packer, their housekeeper, came into the room to retrieve the dirty breakfast dishes. "I assume that both of you scholars know the rest of the legend," she said as she loaded the tray with plates and cups.

"Please tell me," Malcolm said.

"You're English and you don't know?" she taunted him.

"I'm interested to hear what *you* know," he replied.

"My grandmother, who was a scholar of English literature, told me the stories of Arthur. One thing she said again and again was that Arthur would return one day. That's why he has been called 'the once and future king.' "

Jeff considered the phrase, then asked, "What does it mean that he'll come again?"

"Legend has it that he will return at Britain's greatest time of need." She adjusted the tray on her hand. "I guess they gave up on that notion after Hitler and the Blitz of London. That's when Britain needed him the most, I suppose." She balanced the tray and left the room.

Malcolm leaned back in his chair. "You realize, of course, that if he's really Arthur, then we're dealing with a man who has risen from the dead to be here."

"But he's no ghost," Jeff said. "He's flesh and blood."

Malcolm nodded. "That's the thing I can't stop thinking about. He's here in the flesh. How is that possible?"

"*If* it's him, then ... do you think he somehow slipped through time?" Jeff asked.

"You're the one with all the time-travel experience," said Malcolm. "Why don't *you* tell *me*?"

Before Jeff could answer, the phone rang on the server in the corner. He grabbed it. "Hello?" He listened for a minute, mumbled a quick thanks, and hung up. "Uh oh."

Malcolm looked at him, a raised eyebrow.

"Arthur escaped from the hospital this morning."

Malcolm sat up. "How?"

"They were putting him in a van to take him to the Hancock mental hospital and he tossed two of the policemen into a dumpster. He got his clothes and sword from the front of the cab too. He ran off through the field behind the hospital."

"Anybody hurt?"

"No," Jeff answered. "So much for a king's word."

Malcolm smiled. "He promised not to try to escape *last night*. He didn't promise anything about this morning."

Sheriff Hounslow didn't like disruptions to his day. Particularly when the disruptions involved racing around the countryside looking for a large lunatic with a king complex and a very long sword.

Driving in his cruiser, he grabbed his radio handset and barked, "Anybody see anything?"

The radio spat static back at him and then his men reported "negative" from points around town.

"Okay. Keep your eyes peeled. I'm on Rangewood Road on the south side of Dubbs' property heading toward — *Holy Mackerel! There he is!*" Hounslow nearly drove off the road at the sight of Arthur on horseback galloping across Malcolm's land.

"What was that, Sheriff?" someone asked.

"He's on horseback! On the Dubbs property! Surround the place right now!" Hounslow threw the handset down and turned the car onto the first level spot of land he could find. It was enough of a path to get him in the general direction. The car bounced around like a bucking bronco, and he fumbled for the switch to turn on the lights and sirens.

Arthur spurred the horse toward the church ruins about 200 yards ahead. Hounslow did his best to keep up. His car wasn't made for such a rough terrain. He heard his men shouting on the radio but didn't dare take his hands off the wheel to pick up the handset to respond. Suddenly Hounslow's car hopped from the grassy field to a service road that seemed to appear magically in front of him. He laughed low to himself, growing confident as the space between him and his fugitive lessened.

Grabbing the handset he yelled, "He's headed for the church ruins at the center of Dubbs' village!"

The church ruins were actually four stone walls and a make-shift roof that were now enclosed by a wooden construction barricade. Even with the barricade, Hounslow thought the ruins looked more like part of a cathedral than a church, since all he knew of churches were the traditional American kind. He remembered hearing that Malcolm had purchased the ruin from a financially troubled parish in England. *Why* he bought it was beyond Hounslow's imagination. Malcolm had said in a newspaper article that he had hoped to restore the church to how it looked hundreds of years ago.

Hounslow saw Arthur rein in his horse, leap off, and disappear beyond the construction barricades, the sword swinging at his side. Hounslow brought his car to a skidding stop on the loose gravel. He scanned the area and considered his options. He could wait for the rest of his force or go in on his own. He opted for the latter, checking the bullets in his gun before he got out of the car.

The sun shone brightly. Sweat formed on Hounslow's brow as he approached the ruin. He carefully rounded the corner of the barricade, keeping in mind the length of the sword in case the madman decided to swing it at him. No one was there. Hounslow moved past the entrance to an open arched doorway. A large wooden door leaned against the stone wall, waiting to be fitted. Hounslow stepped inside. It was cool and smelled of damp moss, and light streamed through the large, unfinished spaces in the ancient roof. The contrast of light and dark made it hard for Hounslow to see. There were enough shadowed nooks and crannies to keep him on edge.

I should've waited for his back-up, he thought as he looked at the two long rows of fat, round pillars that lined the sanctuary. Arthur, or whatever his name was, could leap out from behind any one of them.

"Okay, pal," Hounslow called out. "Just give yourself up and no one'll get hurt." It was a pointless statement, he knew, if this guy really didn't speak English.

Slowly he made his way farther in to the main sanctuary and looked around. Stones and workers' debris was scattered everywhere. Hounslow noticed that the church actually had tall slots for windows that were now boarded up. High in the rafters, a large blackbird squawked at him, then flapped away noisily until it disappeared through an unfinished part of the south wall.

Hounslow looked left and right, his eyes darting quickly to catch any sign of movement in the shadows. The hard heels of his shoes alternately brushed and clicked against the dirt-covered stone floor. He walked to the far end of the church and stopped in an area where he figured the altar belonged. There in the center sat a large stone block with a slab on top.

He was relieved to hear a car pull up outside. Then another. And a third soon joined them. Car doors slammed and heavy feet crunched on the gravel toward him.

"Sheriff!"

"Inside!" Hounslow shouted back. "Circle the building then *carefully* make your way in to the center. And keep your guns handy!"

Within a minute, Hounslow's patrols were coming toward him from four different entrances — guns poised to shoot. They looked at each other, unsure.

"He has to be around here somewhere," Hounslow said. "Keep looking."

They dispersed as Hounslow checked the perimeter to see if it was possible for Arthur to have raced to any nearby woods.

But there were no nearby woods. Officer Brendan came out of the shadows of the ruins and flinched at the sunlight.

"Well?" Hounslow asked.

"Nothing, Sheriff," Brendan said. "No sign of him."

Hounslow slapped the stone wall. "He couldn't just disappear."

A Jeep approached with Malcolm in the driver's seat. He pulled up next to Hounslow and got out. "What's going on, Sheriff?"

"I tracked our mad king to your church here," Hounslow said.

"So where is he?"

Hounslow looked annoyed. "I don't know. He ran inside and vanished."

"Vanished?" Malcolm repeated with mock skepticism.

"Don't start with me, Malcolm. I don't want a lecture on your theories." He waved at his officers. "Start searching the grounds!"

One by one the officers returned to their cars and drove off in separate directions on the network of service roads through Malcolm's village.

"I assume you'll let me know if he shows up," Hounslow said as he got into his car.

"Eventually."

Hounslow frowned. "He's dangerous, Malcolm," he said, and drove away.

Malcolm walked to the center of the ruin and looked around. *If he's hiding around here somewhere, how can I draw him out?* He remembered a Latin quote from St. Augustine he had learned in college. Maybe if Arthur heard Latin, he'd show himself? Maybe.

"*Intellectus merces est fidei*," Malcolm called out, hoping he said it correctly. *Understanding is the reward of faith.* He waited a moment, then said again, "*Intellectus merces est fidei.*"

Stone grated against stone behind Malcolm. He spun around. The large flat top of the altar moved slightly to the side. Then with a jerk, it moved farther. *He hid inside*, Malcolm thought appreciatively. He grabbed the edge of the top and pushed to help make enough room for Arthur to sit up. Arthur kept a watchful eye on Malcolm as he squeezed out of the large coffin-like box and got to his feet.

"Good for you!" Malcolm exclaimed, glad to see him safe. "Smart thinking!"

Arthur stood on the opposite side of the altar from Malcolm with a stern expression on his face. He said something in Latin.

Malcolm made gestures to show that he didn't understand.

Arthur slowly reached back into the altar and, in a flash, had his sword out of its sheath and pointed under Malcolm's chin.

6

I II III IV V VI VII VIII IX X XI XII

Veni, Verdi, vici!

The unexpected female voice came from a doorway. Malcolm looked past Arthur in astonishment. Arthur spun around just as Jeff and Elizabeth came into the ruins.

"Run, Malcolm," Jeff whispered loudly in his best effort to sound as if he wasn't whispering loudly.

"E pluribus unum!" Elizabeth shouted at Arthur.

Arthur tilted his head. Then he laughed. A chuckle, at first, that built into a full, boisterous laugh, with his held tipped back. He let the sword drop away from Malcolm's chin. Relieved, Malcolm slumped against the stone altar.

"What in the world was *that*?" Malcolm asked.

"I thought shouting at him in Latin might give you a chance to run," Elizabeth explained from a safe distance. "It's all I could think of."

Relaxed now, Arthur sheathed his sword and said something unintelligible to them. They looked at him questioningly. He furrowed his brow as if he suddenly realized how futile it was to speak to them at all. He pointed to the door, then waved his hands to shoo them away.

"He wants us to leave," Jeff said.

"I wonder if we can get him back to the house," Malcolm said.

He followed the statement with a variety of gestures designed to persuade Arthur to come with them.

Arthur folded his arms and shook his head in reply. He shooed them away again.

"We can't leave him here," Malcolm said impatiently. "*We can't leave you here!*" he shouted at Arthur, as if shouting would make him understand.

Arthur pointed at the door.

"What are we going to do?" Jeff asked.

Elizabeth bravely stepped toward Arthur and held out her hand. "*Venire, filiola,*" she said.

Arthur looked puzzled, but his expression softened as he looked at her face, then her outstretched hand, then her face again. He slowly enveloped her hand in his. With a nervous glance to Jeff and Malcolm, she led him out of the ruins into the golden sunlight.

"What did you say to him?" Jeff asked as he and Malcolm followed them out.

"Something my dad used to say to me when I was growing up," she answered. "*Come, child.*"

Jeff and Malcolm looked at each other, impressed.

Elizabeth frowned, "Well, I *think* that's what it meant. I may have just called him my daughter."

○ ○ ○

Outside, the three of them climbed into the Jeep. Arthur stopped several feet away from it. They beckoned him in, but he shook his head no.

"Get in," Malcolm said, gesturing.

Arthur circled the vehicle several times, jabbing parts of it with his hand, looking under it, cautiously touching the tires and doors, then giving it several hard pushes. His face was alive with curiosity.

"Well?" Malcolm asked.

Arthur looked at Malcolm with a coy expression. He then rattled off what might have been questions. Malcolm held up his hands.

Arthur ran his hand along the steering wheel. He seemed to enjoy the way the tires moved when he turned it one way and the other. He pushed on the center and the horn let out a loud blast.

Instantly, Arthur's sword was out, ready to run the beast through.

"No! No!" the three of them shouted.

Arthur put his sword away and walked over to the horse from Malcolm's stable, still waiting patiently by the side of the church ruins. He climbed on and waved Malcolm ahead.

"I guess he wants to follow us," Jeff said.

"I suppose so." Malcolm started the Jeep and away they went, with Arthur behind.

As they drove, Elizabeth called her father on a cell phone and asked him to meet them at Malcolm's cottage right away. "But make sure the police don't follow you," she added before she hung up.

Malcolm nodded. "You're a bright girl."

At Malcolm's cottage, Arthur's inquisitive inspection started all over again. He marveled at the relationship between the switch on the wall and the light on the table. He rifled through Malcolm's books and gawked at Malcolm's computer.

Jeff grabbed his camera to get pictures of Arthur in the new world. He snapped away as Arthur toyed with the gizmos and gadgets of modern living. Jeff turned on the television and Arthur was astounded by the vision and sound. Jeff showed him how the remote control changed the channels. A big mistake. Arthur took it and switched quickly from station to station over and over again. He then settled on a news channel, with a news anchor talking to the camera.

Alan Forde finally arrived and, after giving Elizabeth a rough kiss on the cheek, said hello to Arthur in Latin. Arthur seemed to remember Alan and immediately besieged him with questions.

"He wants to know where the rest of the little man is," Alan said with a laugh. "He can see the front of him, but can't figure out why he can't see the back of him."

"Do you want to try to explain it?" Malcolm asked.

Alan shook his head. "My Latin isn't *that* good."

Arthur grabbed Alan's arm and led him around the room, pointing to various things for Alan to explain.

While they were preoccupied, Malcolm called Mrs. Packer into the room.

"Yes, sir?" she asked, but stopped at the sight of Arthur. "Oh."

"Mrs. Packer, I'd like you to — "

"Aren't you going to introduce me?" she asked.

Malcolm was taken aback by Mrs. Packer's suddenly shy manner, but signaled Alan to bring Arthur over to them. "Alan, please introduce Mrs. Packer to his Highness."

Alan fumbled for the right words, but obviously got them close enough for Arthur to understand. Arthur bowed to Mrs. Packer.

To everyone's surprise, Mrs. Packer blushed and curtsied. "It's nice to meet you," she said. "I'm a big fan of your ... er, legends."

Arthur smiled when Alan translated.

"Would you like his autograph, Mrs. Packer?" Elizabeth giggled.

Mrs. Packer shot her an unappreciative look.

Malcolm cleared his throat. "Mrs. Packer, I wanted you to see him so you'll be able to go downtown to find some less-conspicuous clothes. I don't think it's a good idea for him to wander around in his royal vestments. Do you want a measuring tape?"

Mrs. Packer was all business again and sized Arthur up. "Not needed. I'll remember." She left quickly.

"All right, I think it's time your Highness and I had a talk,"

Malcolm said to Arthur through Alan, and indicated that they should all sit down. "For one thing, what are you doing here?"

"This I know not," Arthur replied with Alan translating. "I have said from whence I come. I know no more. It may be a dream, a cruel joke, or a trick of Merlin's. I know not which."

Malcolm, remembering all he had read earlier in the day, decided to test Arthur. It was still possible that this man was an effective actor or a lunatic. "How could this be a trick of Merlin's when he's disappeared? You haven't seen him in years."

Arthur frowned. "Not in the flesh, no. But I have seen the old wizard sometimes — in my dreams."

"Tell me about your beautiful sword," Malcolm said.

Arthur instinctively put his hand on the hilt. "Everyone in the kingdom knows of this sword. It is *Excalibur.*"

"It must be the one you drew from the stone when you were young," Malcolm said, again testing the man.

Arthur laughed scornfully. "Fie on thee, knave. Excalibur was given to me by the Lady of the Lake!"

"Please, tell me the story," Malcolm asked.

"I once fought a tournament with King Pellinore and was wounded," Arthur began. "Merlin took me to a hermit who bound my wounds and gave me good salves to aid their healing. When I was mended, Merlin and I departed. As we rode into a deep wood, I discerned that I had no sword upon me. Merlin said it was of no consequence, for a greater sword was soon to be mine. Now it came to pass that we came to a lake and in the midst of it I espied an arm clothed in white silk reaching heavenward from the water. In its hand was a sword of surpassing beauty. I was dazzled. Then I saw a damsel on the lake and she came unto me and said that the sword would be mine if I gave her whatsoever gift she asked for. By my faith, I promised to grant her any such gift, for the sword was right wondrous. She said she would make her request at a time of her own choosing and departed, directing me to take a nearby boat and to row to the sword, still held by the hand. I rowed to the place and took the sword by the handle. As I marveled at the weapon and tested its feel, the arm and hand swiftly drew under the water again, leaving barely a ripple. I took Excalibur, for so was the sword named, and returned to land. Many wondrous things have we seen since, Excalibur and I."

"Is this for real?" Jeff said softly to Elizabeth.

Elizabeth nodded. "If the legends are true — yes."

"I'd like to hear the story of how you died," Malcolm said to Arthur, knowing this would make or break the theory he'd been formulating all day.

His request led to a brief and angry exchange between Arthur and Alan. Finally Alan turned to Malcolm. "He resents this interrogation. Who are you to riddle him with questions? How dare you ask him about death?"

"He knows how he died?" Malcolm asked.

"No," Alan answered. "That's why he's so angry. He *hasn't* died. He wants to know if this is some kind of trick or dream or premonition about his battle against Mordred."

Malcolm tugged at his ear thoughtfully. "Well, that's interesting."

"What?" Jeff asked.

"Assuming once again that this man isn't some kind of lunatic and is King Arthur, then we've confirmed one thing. He really did slip through time somehow *before* his last battle with Mordred."

"Are you going to tell him how he dies?" Jeff asked.

"No," Malcolm replied. "Alan, please tell His Majesty that I'm terribly sorry for asking him so many questions. But just as his appearance here is confusing to *him*, it's equally confusing to *us*. This isn't a trick, a dream, or a premonition."

Alan translated the message and Arthur responded.

"What did he say?" Malcolm asked.

"He said that he's very hungry," said Alan.

Malcolm stood up. "Then let's go raid the kitchen."

○ ○ ○

Arthur poked, prodded, and smelled the multiple plates of meat, fruits, and vegetables Malcolm put before him. Eventually he dared a taste and, satisfied that it wouldn't harm him, attacked it all with his bare hands.

"That's disgusting," Elizabeth said.

"At least he's authentic" Alan said, grinning. "Eating utensils like forks weren't known in Europe until four hundred years after Arthur's reign."

"Okay, Malcolm, what are you thinking?" Jeff asked.

Malcolm had been leaning against the kitchen counter, arms folded, his gaze on no fixed point. "This is a problem." Malcolm moved away from the counter and began a slow pace from one end of the kitchen to the other. "Let's say that he *is* Arthur. What's he doing here?"

"He doesn't seem to know," Alan answered.

"That's the problem," Malcolm said. "If *he* doesn't know, then how are *we* supposed to know?"

Jeff snagged a piece of ham from Arthur's plate. Arthur frowned at him. "You're assuming that he's here for a reason. Maybe he's just here because … I don't know … Time hiccupped and brought him here by accident."

"You should know better than anyone that things don't happen simply by accident." Malcolm eyed both Jeff and Elizabeth. They looked at each other self-consciously.

"I had this feeling …" Elizabeth began hesitantly. "When we were stuck in the fog, I got a feeling like I had the night I switched to that other time."

"Fawlt Line," Malcolm muttered as he vigorously paced back and forth. Arthur stopped eating to watch him. "I've been thinking a lot about Fawlt Line. Has anyone ever asked why it's called that?"

"Named after Thaddeus Fawlt back in 1728, I heard," Alan offered.

"That's what I always heard too," Malcolm said. "But I've been studying the history of our town and there's more to it than that. The town's name was originally spelled as *Fault* Line, with a *u*, in the late 1600's, until Thaddeus Fawlt came along and changed the spelling to suit his name. So why *Fault* Line? It's not as if we're on any kind of geographical fault here."

Arthur said something to Alan.

"He wants to know what you're talking about," Alan reported.

"Yes, Malcolm, what are you getting at?" Elizabeth asked.

Malcolm shoved his hands into his pockets. "I believe Fawlt Line is on some sort of *time fault*."

Everyone stared at Malcolm, speechless.

Malcolm turned to Jeff and Elizabeth again. "Your adventure made me do the research. We have over two hundred years of random incidents that when looked at individually can be easily dismissed, but when you put them all together . . ." He spread his hands. "It's *very* strange."

Alan coughed uncomfortably. "Do you really want me to say all that to Arthur?"

"Yes, if you can," Malcolm said. "It might help him to understand. If we're on some kind of time fault, then it's possible that he slipped through. Randomly, perhaps — or for some reason that we haven't sorted out."

Alan began an animated conversation with Arthur.

"Malcolm," Jeff said quietly. "What if you're wrong?"

Malcolm gazed intensely at Arthur as he replied, "Then this man is out of his mind and we're at great risk being near him."

At that moment, Alan finished his explanation.

Arthur looked in wide-eyed disbelief at Malcolm, then threw his head back and laughed loudly for a long time.

II

There & Here

"I don't believe it," Graham Ridley said to his wife from the kitchen table in their English home. Graham put his tea cup down and looked closer at the small article buried in the center of the London newspaper.

"What now?" Anne Ridley asked, sitting down at the table with her freshly made toast.

"Apparently there's a man in America who believes he's King Arthur," Graham said. "It says he mysteriously showed up in a field somewhere dressed to the hilt in a cape, tunic, and tights, speaking Latin, and brandishing a large sword as well."

Anne giggled. "What in the world would Arthur be doing in America?"

"Sightseeing, I suppose. He was found in a small town somewhere in Maryland," Graham said and carefully tore the article out of the paper.

"What are you doing?" Anne asked through another bite of her toast.

Graham chuckled. "I want to show the article to Myrddin. You know how he is about King Arthur."

"Don't torture him, Graham," Anne teased. "He'll want to borrow money for a flight over."

"Borrow from whom? I'm his vicar, not the Prince of Wales,"

he said as he tucked the article into his shirt pocket. "And I may not be his vicar for long."

"Oh, Graham, do stop."

The phone chirped from the front hall. Anne went to answer it.

The wooden chair creaked as Graham sat back and looked out the kitchen window. He gazed at his church — Christ Church of Wellsbridge — an assemblage of thick and uneven stone walls, sloped roofs, and arches of varying sizes that framed the doorways and tall stained-glass windows. Its square 100-foot-high tower had an elegantly spired crown. As best as anyone could tell, the church was at least 600 years old, perhaps older. But in its long history, it had been through several renovations and restructurings. The tower, for example, was modeled after the tower of Magdalen College at Oxford University in deference to the wishes of a wealthy patron who had rescued the financially stricken church in the early 1800's. The oldest part of the church, including the original nave and apse, had recently been cleared away and sent to a buyer in America. *Typical*, Graham had thought at the time. *The Americans appreciate the value of things we've forgotten.*

The people of Wellsbridge certainly didn't value the church. To them it was a neglected monument, which needed restoration again. Subsidence in the foundations left it looking slumped, as if tired, and in danger of being condemned by building inspectors. But this time there wouldn't be a wealthy patron to rescue it. Just the opposite, in fact. The only wealthy patron in the area would love to tear the building down and put in a large "superstore" — much like those American-style factory outlets that had sprung up all over the landscape of England recently.

Years ago, tearing down a house of God like this would have been unthinkable. It seems Christianity in England is deteriorating along with this church's foundation, Graham thought, and sighed. Christ Church of Wellsbridge was ever steadfast, ever faithful, waiting diligently to receive, whether anyone ever came or not. Unfortunately, few people came any more, and Wellsbridge didn't have the population to sustain a church that size — or a church at all. In fact, Wellsbridge was the kind of tiny village tourists pictured on a postcard of England but never made their way to see in person. The high street had a bank, a newsagent, a locally owned grocery shop, and The Rose & The Crown Pub. A small road off the high street led to the rectory, Graham's home for the past three years and, of course, Christ Church. What else was there? A few small cottages and outlying farms. It was just as easy to go north to the cathedral in Wells or south to a church in Glastonbury, churches with more historical value.

Which is precisely why so many people thought the church should be closed and a superstore built in its place, Graham mused. Good for local economy, they kept saying in the village meetings. How could Graham effectively argue against it?

Anne appeared in the doorway. "That was the archdeacon on the phone. He wants to see you right away."

"The archdeacon?" Graham gulped. The archdeacon was the bishop's hatchet man. He was the one who called when there were problems in the parish that the bishop didn't want to deal with. "What have I done now?"

"He didn't say. He asked me to come as well, but I don't dare miss my luncheon with Mrs. Hammond. It'd be the third week in a row and she'd never forgive me."

Graham was aghast. "You told the archdeacon that? You said you couldn't come with me because of lunch with Mrs. Hammond?"

"Not in so many words," Anne said. "But I wouldn't keep him waiting if I were you."

Graham was out the door and speeding his Mini Cooper down the road in less than a minute.

✿ ✿ ✿

"Sit down, sit down." The archdeacon, Neville Vail, gestured to Graham from behind his enormous oak desk.

Graham obeyed, sitting nervously on the edge of a gaudy velvety chair with ornate armrests.

"Tea?"

Graham shook his head. "No, thank you."

"Just as well," he said. "My secretary is away this morning."

Graham wiggled uncomfortably in the chair. Obviously it was made for looks, not comfort.

"I've called you in to talk about Adrian," the archdeacon said.

"Adrian?" Graham was puzzled. "As in, my *son* Adrian?"

"Precisely," the archdeacon said, his bushy eyebrows settling like dark clouds over his eyes.

"What about him?"

"Mostly the embarrassment he's causing you," the archdeacon said. "You will be phoned this afternoon by the headmaster at the Winchester School for Boys. Your son's been suspended."

"Suspended!" Graham croaked. "Whatever for?"

"Poor test results and insubordinate behavior," the archdeacon said. "Neither point should surprise you, Graham. You've known how awful his test results have been, and as for his attitude — well, there's little left to be said about that. Would you like to see the head-master's report? He emailed it to me first thing this morning."

Graham shook his head in disbelief. "Adrian isn't like this."

"Nonsense," the archdeacon snapped. "He's been a source of consternation for you for as long as I've known you."

"Since I became vicar of Christ Church," Graham said softly.

"What are you going to do about him? This simply can't go on."

Graham was dazed. He didn't have the slightest idea of what to do. He had been certain that Adrian's attitude problems and constant mischief-making were the result of the move to Wells-bridge. Prior to that, Graham was the vicar of a church in the urban center of Bristol and, though he and Adrian had the usual father-and-teenage son squabbles, things were all right between them. Graham's assignment to the church in Wellsbridge and the relatively sedate lifestyle there changed all that. Adrian became restless and rebellious. He made friends with a few of the local boys who despised everything that Graham and Anne had held dear. He blatantly disregarded rules about how late he could stay out. Arguments between father and son turned into red-faced shouting matches.

The breaking point came with the church tower incident. Adrian and his friends, in a drunken stupor, created a contest to see who could throw their empty beer bottles the farthest from the top of the church. Adrian scored the highest by not only throwing a bottle far enough to reach the street, but by hitting a car as it passed by. A police car.

Graham and Anne had decided to send Adrian to the school in Winchester, where they had hoped he would get out from under the influence of his local friends. It seemed they had hoped for too much.

Blast this chair. Graham wiggled again.

"With all due respect, Neville, why are *you* telling me about this? Why didn't the headmaster call me directly?" Graham asked.

"The headmaster and I are old school mates and he thought something this sensitive should be passed on for my consideration."

"How thoughtful of him," Graham said.

"Look, Graham, you know how people feel about the vicar and his family. They're to be above reproach. A vicar's house should be kept in order, his family kept under control."

Graham spread his hands in appeal. "I don't know what to do. His mother and I have tried to instill goodness and faith in him. But, like many boys his age, he doesn't seem to believe in anything at all."

"Sort it out," the archdeacon warned, then added for good measure, "The bishop isn't pleased."

"The bishop knows about this?" Graham asked helplessly. He wondered, *Am I the last person in the church hierarchy to know about my son's dismissal?*

"I don't have to tell you how this sort of thing can affect your career."

Graham wiggled again. No, he didn't have to be told.

The archdeacon continued, "And it certainly doesn't help the future of Christ Church."

Graham had been waiting for that statement.

"As you know, we've been discussing it for several months now. Richard Ponsonby has been making offers to the bishop for Christ Church, the rectory, and surrounding acreage. If he succeeds, then . . ." The archdeacon let the rest of the sentence go unspoken. Graham knew what the silence meant. Chances were, if he lost Christ Church, he wouldn't be moved to another. His career was on the precipice. And his son was helping to push him over.

"I don't believe there's anything left to say," the archdeacon announced with a slap of both palms on the desktop. He made as if to stand, but didn't. Graham did. "Your son will be arriving at the Wells Train Station on the eleven-fifty."

Adrian squeezed his luggage into the back seat of the Mini then sat down silently in the passenger seat. At fifteen years old, his body was still in an awkward growth stage and his legs didn't seem to know where to go in the small car. Graham pulled away from the front of the train station and into the noonday traffic. It was early for the tourist season, but Wells was unusually congested.

"So?" Graham asked when they cleared town and headed for Wellsbridge.

"So?"

"I think an explanation of some sort is in order," Graham said.

Adrian scrubbed his chin for a moment, as if considering his answers. Finally, he said, "Look, Dad, the fact is, I hated it there and couldn't be bothered to get along with anybody, all right? That's it. Full stop." Adrian slumped down into his seat and bit at a fingernail.

"Well, that's just grand, isn't it?" Graham said with clenched anger. "You couldn't be bothered. All that money spent on your private school fees and you couldn't be bothered. Your mother spending night after sleepless night worrying about you and you couldn't be bothered. My reputation as a vicar going down the toilet and you couldn't be bothered. Then, by all means, tell me what might motivate you to *be* bothered?"

Adrian folded his arms. "Not much. I mean, what's the point?"

"What's the *point*?" Graham suddenly shouted. "The point *is* that you need to straighten yourself out, *that's* the point! I'm a vicar and your antics could very well cost me my job!"

Adrian didn't say anything for a moment. Then he spoke so softly that Graham almost missed it. "So?" Adrian asked.

"So!" Graham nearly lost control of the car.

Adrian didn't speak.

"Is that what this is all about? You've been thrown out of school to come home and tell me that there's no point to my job?" Graham asked.

"It's not as if you *enjoy* what you do, Dad. Wellsbridge is the end of the earth. So maybe it's time you got a new job," Adrian said calmly.

"Get your head out of the clouds, Adrian. Enjoyment has nothing to do with it. I'm *called* to my job. That's what being a vicar is. A calling. And if it takes me to places like Wellsbridge, then that's God's business."

"Yeah, right," Adrian said. "The *bishop's* business, you mean."

Graham prayed for patience. "This conversation has nothing to do with the problem at hand, Adrian."

"Doesn't it?"

"No, because *you're* the problem at hand. We should be talking about you," Graham said. "I don't understand what's happened. You seem determined to make our lives miserable. What happened to that nice young boy we once knew? You used to be so kind and responsible — a good Christian boy, a boy any vicar would be proud to have as a son. *What happened?*"

Adrian bit at another nail. "I asked myself: What's the point? What's the point whether or not I do well in school? What's the point whether you're vicar of Christ Church in Wellsbridge or not? What's the point of *anything*?"

"The point is …" Graham began carefully. "The point is that we're here to … we need to find our place in this world and … to serve God … and to love our neighbors and …" Graham's answer was so lacking in conviction that he couldn't finish it.

"See? *You* don't even know anymore," Adrian said. "When's the last time you believed anything you were doing? It's a joke. You're a career priest. You don't believe there's a point any more than I do!"

His son's words stung Graham at the most tender part of his heart. Was he a career priest — worried mostly about his position in the church — or was he there to serve God in whatever capacity God chose?

What do I believe?

9

I II III IV V VI VII VIII IX X XI XII

"I think he's looking older," Malcolm said to Alan. They were look-ing out at Arthur from the French doors in Malcolm's study. Arthur was dressed in the modern clothes that Mrs. Packer had bought for him, walking around the garden with hands clasped behind his back and head hung low. He'd been with them for a full day now and in that short time his hair had gone grayer and the lines on his face deeper.

"I agree," Alan said. "But what can we do for him?"

Malcolm turned away from the doors, his brow furrowed. "I wish I knew."

"Do you believe he's King Arthur?" Alan asked.

Malcolm looked at Alan thoughtfully, then nodded. "Do you?"

"If he isn't, then he's a remarkable fraud," Alan said. "I thought I knew Latin well, but he uses words in an authentic context — in a way that couldn't have been picked up from a text book. It *sounds* right."

Malcolm smiled at him and opened his mouth to ask a question.

Alan held up his hand. "Don't ask me how or why he's here in our time. I have no idea. But I've seen enough around this town to believe that the impossible is possible and that there's usually a reason behind it. He's here — and we have to help him."

Questions hung in the air between them. How could they help him? What could they do for a man who slipped through time for reasons *he* didn't even know? What was his mission? What part did they play in it?

"I think it's disgraceful," Mrs. Packer said as she entered with a tray of tea.

"Disgraceful?" Malcolm asked.

"All this hand-wringing and worrying. It's perfectly obvious what you have to do," she said and put the tray on the table with a noticeable rattle of cups.

"We're on pins and needles, Mrs. Packer," Malcolm said.

"You need to get him to England."

Malcolm and Alan looked at her quizzically.

She put her hands on her hips impatiently. "I've told you what my grandmother said. If Arthur is back, then he's come back to help Britain in its greatest time of need."

"How is this Britain's greatest time of need?" Malcolm inquired.

"How am I supposed to know?" Mrs. Packer cried out. "But getting him to Britain makes a lot more sense than standing around here waiting for something to happen!"

Just then the French doors opened and Arthur stepped in. Through Alan he said, "Take me to the church."

Arthur kept his eyes closed as they drove him to the church in the Jeep. "I like this cart not!" he shouted over the wind and the roar of the motor. When they arrived, he got out on wobbly legs and said that it was against nature for a cart to move without the aid of horses.

"It has horses," Malcolm said with a laugh. "But they're under the hood."

Inside the dark ruin, Arthur went to the stone table, crossed himself, and knelt down.

Malcolm and Alan looked at each other, shrugged, and also knelt to pray.

A half an hour later, Arthur crossed himself again and stood up. He turned to face Malcolm and Alan and announced that he could bear it no longer.

"Bear what?" Malcolm asked.

"This waiting and doing nothing!" he said through Alan. "While I wear these strange clothes, pace in your gardens, and are entertained by your enchantments, Mordred is stealing my kingdom!"

Malcolm held up his hand. "I have a theory about that, your Highness. If Mordred took over your kingdom, then all of history would change since he didn't succeed originally."

Arthur cocked an eyebrow. "Didn't he? Are you saying that he was defeated in our battle?"

Malcolm chose his words carefully. "I can honestly say that, yes, he was defeated. But it would be wrong to say anything else."

"Pray, what is your theory, sir?" Arthur asked.

"Since history *hasn't* changed, then I can only assume that Mordred hasn't taken over your kingdom. I suspect that your time has been frozen by your absence and will resume when you return."

"That sounds absurd," Alan said before he translated what Malcolm had said.

Malcolm nodded. "So is his being here. But he is and I can only assume that somehow time fractured or bent in order for it to happen. Maybe the hours he spends with us will only seem like seconds in his time."

Alan nodded. "It sounds impressive, even if it's wrong." He translated the message to Arthur.

Arthur shook his head, bewildered. "I understand not how this can be, yet I hope you are right. For if Mordred takes my kingdom, then all is lost. He is a brutally cruel man. He tortures the helpless for sport. He is without a knight's honor or a noble-man's virtue. He is an evil shadow on the face of my land." Arthur suddenly pounded his fist on the stone slab. "I must serve my purpose here and go home!"

Malcolm tugged at his ear with a resolute look in his eyes. "Then let's get you to England so you can do both."

10

As an initial punishment for getting thrown out of school, Graham made Adrian help him with his work around Christ Church. They spent the afternoon cutting the grass and clearing away the weeds from the stone sidewalk and along the side of the church. Afterward, with a shovel, pick, and wheelbarrow, they trudged around to the south side of the church where the oldest section had once stood. Parts of the ruin still remained, but mostly as random piles of stones.

"Wow," Adrian exclaimed. "This looks different."

Graham agreed. After the ruins had been carted off to America, he had begun to tear the ground up with a tiller. "I want to plant another garden here," he told Adrian. "Maybe I'll put in a couple of benches and make this a garden for meditation."

Adrian leaned against the shovel handle, now sticking up out of the dirt. "Some American really paid *money* for that old wreck of a building? Who was he, someone with more dollars than sense?"

"He's English, actually, but living in America. The archdeacon worked out the details with him," Graham said as he thrust his shovel into the dirt and began to dig. "I only met him for a moment. He's some sort of history enthusiast. He's building a village dedicated to time."

"Like St. Fagan's," Adrian said. "It's a village outside Cardiff that has farmhouses and shops and schools — all from different periods of history. I went there on a school trip. Remember?"

Graham didn't. His attention went to several chunks of stone littering the ground along the church wall. He peered up to see where they'd come from, and saw cracks and holes near the edge of the roof. More evidence of the building's subsidence, he knew.

"What's that?" Adrian asked.

"Debris," Graham said and returned to his digging. "The church's foundation is sinking."

"Isn't that dangerous?"

Graham nodded. "It's not dangerous to the congregation, but it's dangerous to *me*. If the building inspectors find out before I can get the money to restore it, they'll close the church."

"How much money do you have so far?"

"Not a penny," Graham said helplessly.

"Then why bother?" Adrian asked. "It's not as if it has any value. You have three blue-haired old ladies who attend services regularly. Maybe a couple of walking tourists who got lost. And Myrddin, who most people think is mad."

"That's not the point," Graham said.

Adrian made as if he didn't hear him. "The church doesn't even have any important history connected to it. What does it have other than that bizarre stone altar?"

The stone altar at the head of the church was literally that: an altar carved ornately from solid Somerset rock. One historian guessed from the design that it might have been made as early as the fifth century.

"It must be worth a lot of money. The archdeacon didn't even let it go to the American."

"No, he sent the stone priest's table instead. He wants the altar for the museum in Wells," Graham explained.

"There you are, then," Adrian said. "You could lose this church and no one would notice."

Graham felt deflated. "Thank you, son. I appreciate your support."

Graham and Adrian dug silently for a moment. Graham lost himself in the depressing situation that stood before him. How could he solicit funds for the restoration of the church without drawing undue attention to the church's condition? For he had no doubt that once the word got out, Richard Ponsonby would make his move to close the church and secure it for his super-store site.

As if on cue, Richard Ponsonby himself pulled up in his Ferrari. Graham groaned. Ponsonby was one of the new breed of merciless businessmen who did whatever was necessary to fulfill their ambitions. British diplomacy and a sense of fair play were not part of his conduct. Heaven help whomever got in the way. That included Graham for trying to block Ponsonby's efforts to tear down Christ Church.

"Our beloved vicar in backbreaking labor!" Ponsonby said heartily as he climbed out of the car, dressed smartly in tailored trousers and complementary sports jacket. "And people say our church leaders are never down to earth."

"Hello, Mr. Ponsonby," Graham said. He tossed a shovelful of dirt onto the chunks of stone that had fallen from the wall before Ponsonby could see them.

"Adrian, you're back from school." Ponsonby smiled at Graham's son.

Adrian nodded silently.

Graham had no doubt that Ponsonby knew everything there was to know about Adrian's dismissal.

"I see your father has wasted no time in putting you to work," Ponsonby said. "Good for him. I'm a big believer in hard work. It was hard work that gave me my first million before I was twenty-seven."

Other people's hard work, Graham thought.

"I thought it only sporting to let you know that I put in a new offer to the bishop for this church and lands," Ponsonby said.

Graham lifted another shovelful of dirt and threw it onto the remaining chunk of stone. "How interesting," he said. *He's riding on the coattails of Adrian's dismissal. He knows it's a perfect time to impress the bishop that the vicar of Christ Church should be removed and the church torn down*, Graham thought.

"You can't blame me," Ponsonby asserted. "It's a terrible misuse of resources for you to spend so much time caring for a church that isn't needed in this area."

"I appreciate your deep concern about the church's resources and my time, Mr. Ponsonby. However, I would respectfully submit that churches are needed in *every* area. It's more superstores that aren't needed, I suspect," Graham said with great restraint.

Ponsonby chuckled. "Well, now, that's where we'll have to disagree. What do *you* think, Adrian? Are you for progress or against it?"

Adrian stopped digging. He chose the words for his answer carefully. "Frankly, it doesn't matter to me one way or the other. I'm not sure that a superstore represents progress any more than I believe that this church represents anything more than wishful thinking from the past."

Ponsonby clapped his hands. "An excellent answer! I believe you've knocked us both with that one. Don't you agree, Graham?"

Graham gazed at his son. "He's good at that."

"You have a bright boy here," Ponsonby continued. "He's quick on his feet."

"Not very quick with that shovel though," Graham said.

"Ho, ho. Are you going to look for a job now that you're out of school, Adrian?"

"I don't know."

"I'd be pleased if you'd come to see me," Ponsonby said. "I could use someone like you on my estate. That is, if your father wouldn't mind." He turned to Graham. "You wouldn't be intimidated if your son came to see me, would you, Graham?"

Graham clenched the shovel handle and stabbed it into the thick earth. "Intimidated? Why would that intimidate me?"

"Excellent!" Ponsonby said. "Then you don't mind. Good. Come and visit me, Adrian, and we'll see what we can do for you."

"Thanks. Maybe I will."

"Or maybe you won't," Graham muttered. "He's out of school for the moment, but that doesn't mean he'll stay out of school."

Ponsonby scoffed, "School never helped me in any of my business. It's what you have instinctively *up here*." He tapped the side of his head. "That's what matters."

"Perhaps that worked for you, but I doubt if — "

Ponsonby cut Graham off. "I only want to talk with him, Graham. I want to see what he's made of. It certainly won't do him any harm. All things considered, it might do him a world of good."

There was something about the way he said "all things considered" that made Graham want to attack Ponsonby with his shovel. "All things considered" meant "Considering what a rotten job you've done with your son."

"Well, Dad?" Adrian asked.

Graham sighed. "It's up to you, son."

11

I II III IV V VI VII VIII IX X XI XII

"Myrddin?" Graham shouted as he tapped on the splintered wooden door.

From somewhere inside the old ramshackle cottage he heard Myrddin call out, "Hullo, Graham. Come in. I've made you some tea."

Graham opened the door and stepped in. "Did you? But how did you know I was coming? I didn't know myself until a few minutes ago."

"Sit down, sit down," Myrddin said impatiently. "We have much to talk about."

Myrddin was in the tiny kitchen, separated from the main room by a counter. The teapot rattled and water splashed. Graham sat down in a thick oak chair that might've been a couple of hundred years old. He didn't know its age — any more than he knew the age of anything in the old place. It was timeless, much like Myrddin himself. From where he sat, he could see Myrddin's head bobbing up and down as he prepared the tray of tea. His wild, white hair danced around like a loose halo. His frock hung on him like a monk's habit on a skeleton.

With thin, shaking hands, Myrddin put the tray on a small table that served as both a server and desk. "Things are happening, Graham," he said, a thin smile stretching across his bony face. His cheeks were flushed and his blue eyes were childlike in their alertness. That's what impressed Graham more than anything. Though his angular skeletal body and waxed-paper skin made him look like a walking corpse, his eyes betrayed a soul that was quickened, certainly more alive than people much younger. Myrddin leaned forward across the table and said again, "Things are happening!"

Graham poured the tea and said sadly, "They certainly are. My church is about to be declared a health hazard."

Myrddin waved the comment away. "Minor repairs. I'm talking about — "

"Not minor, Myrddin," Graham interrupted. "It's worse than you think. The foundation is sinking. If Ponsonby ever finds out just how badly the church is damaged, he'll have his superstore in no time at all. It's awful. And I haven't even told you about Adrian. He was thrown out of school. I was told by the *archdeacon*."

"Yes, yes, of course. But I'm talking something more important than that," Myrddin said.

Graham frowned. "I'm sorry, but my church and my family are falling apart and I'll likely be out of a job by this time next year. I fail to see what could be more important."

"How about a miracle, eh? How about something that will change the way we look at the world?" Myrddin said with *that* look in his eyes. In three years, Graham came to know that look well. It said that the old man was up to something.

"What are you talking about?" Graham asked, not sure he wanted to hear.

Myrddin held up a bony finger that looked like an exclamation mark. "The return of Arthur!" he announced.

Graham stirred his tea. "Oh, you've seen the newspaper then."

"Newspaper? No, I haven't. What about it?"

Graham fished in his shirt pocket for the article he had torn out of the paper earlier. He was disappointed to realize it suddenly wasn't there. "I must've left it in the other shirt pocket. The article said that someone claiming to be King Arthur showed up in some small town in America. I thought you'd be interested."

"When? When did he show up?" Myrddin asked.

Graham sipped his tea. "A couple of days ago."

Myrddin clasped his hands in childlike delight. "I knew it! I knew it!"

"Calm down," Graham said.

"But Graham — "

"Anne told me not to mention it to you. She's said you would get yourself in a state."

"And why not?" Myrddin exclaimed. "King Arthur returned. It's perfect, absolutely perfect!"

Graham was chagrined. "I don't see what's so perfect about it. He's in America."

"A slight hiccup, I'm sure." Myrddin scratched at his scruffy beard as he paced around the room. He was lost in his own thoughts. "The time was right. I knew it. I could feel it. I wonder what his plan is. I wonder how he'll get here."

"I doubt he'll get anywhere. Don't Americans lock up crazy people like that?"

Myrddin's his bushy eyebrows gathered on his forehead. "Do they?"

"Probably," Graham said, then added affectionately, "You wouldn't stand a chance there, you know. One look at you and they'd have you in a padded room."

"Do you think I'm crazy?" Myrddin asked in earnest.

Graham smiled and said warmly, "I think you're certifiable. Now draw deep into your well of wisdom and tell me what I'm going to do about Ponsonby and my church."

"Do you know what I think?" Myrddin asked. "I think you should forget about him. Our horizons just got bigger. Bigger than Ponsonby and your church ... even your problems with Adrian."

"Because King Arthur is coming back."

"Exactly! England needs — "

Graham interrupted him with a groan. "Sometimes I think I'd feel terribly sorry for you if I didn't consider you such a good friend."

"You think I'm a lunatic. What makes me such a good friend?"

Graham lifted his drink. "You make a good cup of tea."

12

I II III IV V VI VII VIII IX X XI XII

Ponsonby Manor was a sprawling gray seventeenth-century manor house allegedly built by King George the Third as a measure of gratitude to Robert Ponsonby. No one knew why the king said thank you to Robert Ponsonby in such a grandiose way. People at the time speculated that it had something to do with questionable business dealings done on behalf of the king.

A stiff servant, with a face as gray as the stone entrance, greeted Adrian and led him quietly to Ponsonby's "study." *This room is as big as our entire house*, Adrian thought as he sat down in a plush wingback chair. The study had everything Adrian expected a rich man's study to have: Dark cherrywood paneling with ornately carved bookshelves stuffed with carefully arranged leather binders, a desk the size of a small van, antique furniture tastefully displayed on several Persian carpets, tapestries, the obligatory globe of the world, a large fireplace topped with two very long crossed swords and family crest, and huge windows with warped glass, distorting the outside world.

"I'm glad you came to see me, Adrian," Ponsonby said as he strode into the room. He shook Adrian's hand vigorously. "It shows ambition on your part."

Adrian tried to sound indifferent. "It was either this or stay home and watch the telly with Mum and Dad."

Ponsonby laughed as he circled his enormous desk and set-tled in his burgundy leather chair. "You're a clever lad."

Adrian smiled politely. "Look, Mr. Ponsonby, I appreciate the offer of a job, but I think — "

"Did I offer you a job? I thought I had asked you to come see me about one. But I don't remember making an offer." Ponsonby gave Adrian a coy look.

"Sorry. You're right," Adrian flushed. "But before we go any further — "

"I understand that you like to toy with cars," Ponsonby said.

"Sure. I work on them when I get a chance."

"I'm in need of someone who'll take care of my cars. I have a few that I'm particularly fond of. Do you want to see them?" Ponsonby was on his feet again.

"If you want me to."

"No, Adrian," Ponsonby corrected him. "Say yes because *you* want to. We won't get anywhere if you're not firm. Reminds me of someone else we both know. Now do you want to see my cars or not?"

Adrian was so surprised by the sudden rebuke that he could only nod, "Yes, sir."

"Much better. Follow me."

They walked silently from the study, back down the hall into the large foyer, and out through the front door. Crossing the cobble-stoned semi-circular driveway, they approached a long building that looked like a stable, with ten square doors along the front. They stepped though a pedestrian door within one of the larger doors, where a row of cars sat in regal sophistication under fluorescent lights. Adrian's mouth fell open at the sight. Ponsonby gestured to each car as they walked past.

"This red one is a Ferrari 410 Super America. Only five in the country," he said. "This, in British racing green, is an E-type Jaguar, V–12 model. This beauty is my Rolls Royce Silver Ghost. I believe you'll recognize my Aston-Martin DB–4. And in a specially created navy blue shade, my Bristol Beaufighter. It's hand-built."

"These are all yours?" was all Adrian could manage to say.

Ponsonby nodded. "I'm not one for driving cars myself. But I love to look at them. And they certainly make an impression on visitors."

"I'm sure they do," Adrian croaked. His mouth had gone dry.

"Do you know why I bought these cars?" Ponsonby asked.

"Why?"

"Because I could *afford* to buy them. When I put down cash for a car like, say, that Ferrari without feeling so much as a pinch or a tingle of concern that there'll be enough left over for other things, it reminds me of who I am. It reminds me that I've reached a point in my life when I can have what I want when I want it. Do you know what that feels like?"

"No, sir."

Ponsonby lips curled into a cruel smile. "Of course you don't. And you won't so long as you persist in being a failure."

It felt like Ponsonby had suddenly slapped him in the face. *Persist in failure.*

Ponsonby held up a hand. "The truth can be cruel, but never should it be ignored. Listen to me. There are people who would give their left arms to hear what I'm telling you for free. Don't persist in being a failure."

"I don't understand," Adrian said.

"What was that business at school, eh? Bad test results, stupid pranks ... For what? What will that do for you, for your future? Nothing. When I was your age — no, don't look at me like that — when I was your age, I was working hard and thinking about the future. Why? Because I knew that by the time I reached the age of forty I wanted to be able to walk into *my* garage and look at cars like these. Cars that I *own*."

"But you were born rich."

"I was born into a rich family," Ponsonby said.

"What's the difference?"

Ponsonby lips pressed into a cruel smile once again. "The difference is that my father insisted that each one of his children must prove themselves. He pitted us against one another to gain favor for the top position in his will when he died. I won."

"But I don't think I'd want to base my life on acquiring cars," Adrian said.

"Then don't," Ponsonby replied simply. "But what *do* you want to base your life on? Make up your mind and then go for it. Take all you can from life and don't give anything back. Determine your plan. If it includes school, then do your absolute best at school. Not because it's what your parents want or because you think it's the right thing to do, but because it suits your plan — because it's the thing *you* want to do. I think you're smarter than you like to let on. I look at the fire in your eyes and do you know what I see?"

"What?"

"I see myself at your age. You're trying to decide the meaning of life, your purpose, what you believe in. I'm here to help you decide." Ponsonby casually leaned over to the rear fender of the Rolls Royce and brushed at a tiny piece of something.

Adrian was overwhelmed. His brain seemed to be working in slow motion. "Hang on. You want to help *me* decide?"

"I can't stand waste, Adrian. And I think it would be a waste for you to ... I shouldn't say it."

"Say what?"

Ponsonby shuffled awkwardly. But it looked contrived. "I think it would be a waste for you to wind up like your father." He exhaled as if a huge weight had been taken from his shoulders. "There. My cards are on the table. I look at you and I see myself thirty years ago. My heart goes out to you. I want to rescue you."

Adrian felt numb now. "Rescue me how?"

"By offering you that job. I want you to help take care of my cars."

"But ... why me?" Adrian stammered.

"Why *not* you?"

"Because ... well, I don't know, really, except ..."

Ponsonby frowned at him and spoke irritably, "Adrian, if you insist on continuing with this imitation of your father, I'll retract the offer and send you home. I'm saying this only once. But, unlike a lot of offers you'll get, you should know now that this one may change the direction of your life. You have the potential to stand in your own garage and look at your own collection of cars — or *whatever* you fancy. Or you could wind up a good but trampled man trying to save things that aren't worth saving. Like that old church of your father's. So ... what are you going to do?"

13

The next morning saw King Arthur having his first modern shower, which Mrs. Packer refused to help with, and a trim of his hair and beard, which Mrs. Packer was more than happy to help with. "As scruffy as you look, I can't imagine what Guinevere saw in you!" she said as she cut away, knowing he couldn't understand her.

Jeff showed Arthur how to dress in a suit, but gave up on getting him to wear a tie.

Malcolm applauded when Arthur made his appearance at the breakfast table. Elizabeth, who had just arrived with her father, looked curiously at Arthur, then Malcolm. "What's going on here, Malcolm? Why do you have him dressed up like that?"

"Well, I can't take him to the British Embassy looking like ... like ..."

"King Arthur," Jeff finished for him.

"Right," Malcolm said. Malcolm took a bite of his grapefruit.

"The British Embassy!" Elizabeth exclaimed. "You mean, the one in Washington, D.C.?"

"We can't get him to England without a passport," Malcolm said. "We'll fly down in my plane."

Elizabeth watched as Arthur attacked everything on the breakfast table. "Apart from his table manners, he's a pretty good-looking man."

"Particularly when you consider that he's over a thousand years old," Jeff observed.

Alan, who'd been lost in his own thoughts, suddenly asked, "How are you going to get a passport for him?"

"I'll take him to the passport office and explain that we have a British subject who needs a passport."

"And, presumably, they'll ask what happened to his passport — was it lost, destroyed, stolen? If you admit he never had a passport, then they'll want proof of his British citizenship. What will you show them? He has no birth certificate or any of the other I.D."

Malcolm frowned. "Good point. Silly of me not to think of it."

"What are we going to do?" Jeff asked.

"You're going to need a miracle for this," Alan said. "In this day and age, with security being what it is, I can't imagine how you'd navigate the bureaucracy to come up with a passport."

Malcolm stood up and paced for a moment. Then he brightened up and said, "I think I have an idea." He left the room. They nibbled their breakfasts in silence. Ten minutes later, Malcolm returned. "Right! Let's go."

"What did you do?" Jeff asked.

"I talked to someone who can work a miracle."

They stood to leave, but then Alan paused as he was putting on his jacket and asked, "Are you going to drug him?"

"What?" Malcolm responded. "Drug him? Why?"

"You saw how he was in the Jeep yesterday. How's he going to react to your plane?"

✿ ✿ ✿

Arthur shouted at the top of his lungs.

"We should have drugged him," Malcolm admitted as he guided the twin-engine plane into the skies and south toward Washington.

"Told you so," Alan said, then turned to Arthur and spoke in Latin. "Your Majesty! Look at me! Fix your eyes on me!"

Arthur stopped shouting and looked wildly at Alan. "How is this possible? How can we fly as the birds fly?"

"It's like all of the other machines you have seen," Alan explained. "This one allows us to fly."

Arthur looked at him with childlike amazement. "Will you teach me how you do it? What a marvel this will be for my people!"

"I don't think that would be a very good idea," Alan said. "Meanwhile, maybe you should close your eyes and sit back for the rest of the trip. It won't be so frightening that way."

"You dare to say I'm frightened?" Arthur challenged him.

"Of course not, your Majesty." Alan turned forward again and gave Malcolm a knowing look. "He says he's not frightened."

Arthur carefully leaned toward the small round window and peered out. Below him were scattered pillows of clouds and rolling green farmlands.

He shouted again.

○ ○ ○

The drive from Reagan Airport gave Arthur an instant education in the hustle and bustle of a city — in this case, the nation's capital. Malcolm purposefully played the tour guide and took him past Washington's most important sites. Arthur's head seemed to turn a complete 360 degrees as he looked and pointed at everything from the crowds of people at the crosswalks and traffic lights to the Greek-style architectural tributes to Lincoln and Jefferson and, of course, the Washington Monument.

The British Passport and Visa Office wasn't part of the British Embassy as Malcolm had thought. It was about 100 yards away, down Massachusetts Avenue. It was housed in a nondescript building with a small reception area and beleaguered Visa officers rushing to-and-fro behind thick security windows. Alan spoke to the receptionist and was told to sit down. They did.

"Well," Alan said. "Are you going to explain how this miracle is supposed to happen?"

Malcolm picked up an old magazine. "An old friend from my days at Oxford."

"A student? An instructor?"

"A fellow researcher," Malcolm replied. "I spent a year at Oxford for a joint British and American government project. My government contact had been Simon Jenkins. He became a good friend, and — "

"Sir, if you'll *please* sit down!" came an exasperated cry.

Malcolm and Alan looked up. Arthur was pointing and gesturing at the thick security glass separating the reception area from the visitors. Alan leapt to his feet and, taking Arthur by the arm, guided him away from the harried woman.

Arthur jabbered at him in Latin. Alan answered, trying to explain about the glass. They sat down.

"The sooner we get out of here, the better I'll feel," Alan said.

Malcolm agreed, then said quietly, "Look, Alan, some of my work was in the Intelligence field and — "

"Malcolm Dubbs!" a man called out.

All three men looked toward a doorway, where a man in a loose-fitting suit stood.

Malcolm went to him. "Hello, Colin." The two men shook hands.

Colin Jenkins laughed casually. "You haven't changed at all. I'm so glad you rang," he said in a thick British accent. He looked at Alan and Arthur expectantly.

"Oh," Malcolm said, remembering himself, and gesturing for Alan and Arthur to approach. "I'd like you to meet Alan Forde and Arthur ... er, Arthur Pendragon."

Colin shook hands with Alan but hesitated when he took Arthur's hand. "Arthur *Pendragon*? Very interesting. A descendent of King Arthur, I assume?" Colin chuckled. Arthur stared at him incomprehensibly.

Malcolm cleared his throat. "Thank you for seeing us."

"You'd better come in," Colin said, and guided them down

through labyrinth of halls to a small office deep within the building. He gestured for them to sit in the institutional-green chairs while he sat behind a small metal desk. "It seems like yesterday that we were locked up in the Bodleian library working on . . ." He glanced at Alan and Arthur. ". . . *That project*. What an exhilarating time. I think about it often."

Malcolm smiled. "I think of *you* often. It was a delight to learn that you're working here in Washington."

"A temporary assignment, doing research for *you-know-who.*"

Arthur, obviously impatient with all the chatting, suddenly asked Alan if this man would help them get to England.

Colin was surprised. "Was that Latin? Good heavens, I haven't heard anything like it since I was at University. Where's he from?"

"England, but he only speaks Latin," Malcolm said, then added with a whisper, "He's a little eccentric that way."

"Curious," Colin said. Then, with a lot of stammering, Colin asked Arthur what he was doing in America.

Arthur unleashed his answer in a flood of words.

Colin held up his hands in surrender. "Whoa, wait. Slow down. What's he saying?"

Malcolm explained, "As I told you on the phone, we're in a difficult situation. Arthur's a British subject but doesn't have any identification to prove it. We're trying to get him back to England and can't."

Colin eyed Malcolm warily. "Don't you have government contacts to help with your situation?"

"You're my contact, Colin."

"I see. So, who are you working for these days, Malcolm?"

"Working for?" Malcolm asked.

Colin suddenly shook his head. "Sorry. Inappropriate of me to ask. You don't have to say."

"Hold on, Colin. It's not what you think," Malcolm said,

suddenly certain that Colin thought they were working for the government on a top secret operation. "I'm not working for anyone. This is *my* problem. I need a British passport for Arthur, that's all, and don't believe I can get one going the conventional route."

Colin nodded. "I saw the new directives."

"New directives?"

"Red tape on all sides. I understand completely."

"I'm not sure you do," Malcolm said.

Colin winked at Malcolm. "Look, I haven't forgotten what you did for me in Berlin. I'll be happy to help." He stood up. "We'll need photos of him, of course. And the right forms. Wait here, please." He left the room.

Alan and Arthur spoke, then Alan turned to Malcolm. "He wants to know what we're doing."

"We needed a miracle," Malcolm said. "It looks like God has given us the British Secret Service."

Alan looked astonished. "What kind of government project were you doing at Oxford?"

Malcolm shot Alan a wry look.

14

I II III IV V VI VII VIII IX X XI XII

Sheriff Hounslow and two of his officers were waiting for Malcolm, Alan, and Arthur when they stepped from the plane onto the tarmac.

"Hello, Sheriff." Malcolm forced a smile. "What brings you here?"

Hounslow jabbed a finger at Arthur. "He does. We've been looking all over for him. Imagine my surprise to find out that he's with you."

Arthur's entire body stiffened, as if he might lunge at the sheriff. Alan put a restraining hand on Arthur's arm.

"I don't understand. You're acting as if he's a fugitive," Alan said.

"In a way he is. The doctors at the hospital want him transported to Hancock because his violent behavior poses a threat to the public — "

"Now, Sheriff, that's nonsense and you know it."

"I know no such thing," Hounslow snapped. "My car's going to be in the shop for a week from chasing this lunatic across your property."

"That's right. *My* property."

"Exactly. So maybe I should take you in as an accessory."

"Accessory to what?"

"To ... harboring a fugitive. Resisting arrest."

"That's ridiculous. Where's your warrant?" Malcolm demanded. "At worst, you might accuse him of stealing a horse — but it was *my* horse and I won't press charges. Now, if you'll excuse us, we're going back to my house."

"You can go back to your house, but our Highness here is going back to the hospital. I don't want this madman wandering the streets of Fawlt Line."

"Sheriff, he won't be wandering anywhere. He'll be with me. I've made plans for him to — "

"Don't bother explaining, Malcolm. He's going to the hospital first while we figure out who's going to pay for the damage to my car."

"Good heavens, *I'll* pay for the damage to your car. You have my word. And, after tomorrow, you won't have to worry about him. He won't be here."

"We'll see about that," Hounslow said and reached for Arthur. "Come along. We don't want a scene."

Arthur didn't move.

Hounslow groaned. "He's not going to be difficult, is he? Tell him in whatever gibberish he's speaking to come along quietly."

Malcolm began, "Richard — "

"Let's go, your Eminence." Hounslow gave Arthur's arm a tug.

Arthur quickly jerked his arm, knocking Hounslow off balance. He fell to the ground with a thud.

"Arthur! No!" Malcolm shouted.

The two officers jumped at Arthur, but he anticipated their move and quickly grabbed one of the officers by the shirt collar and swung him around with a bone-crunching thump into the other.

"Stop, Arthur, stop!" Alan yelled to Arthur in Latin.

At the sound of the Latin, Arthur turned to Alan. One of the officers leapt onto his back. Arthur toppled and fell to the tarmac. In an instant, the other officer was also on top of him. Hounslow, recovering himself, joined in the fray.

"Stop!" Malcolm shouted again and again. "He doesn't understand!"

The three men managed to get Arthur turned over onto his stomach and wrenched his hands to a position where they could snap the handcuffs on his wrists.

"Sheriff, listen to me!"

Hounslow and his men dragged Arthur to the car, being careful not to let him get a proper footing, and dumped him into the back of the first police cruiser. He fought against them but they managed to get the door closed. Arthur roared from inside.

Hounslow checked the torn knee on his trousers, then looked accusingly at Malcolm. "Look at what he did. This isn't helping his case, you know. Attacking a policeman."

"He didn't attack you. He simply doesn't understand," Malcolm said.

"Then I guess he'll learn really fast, won't he?" Hounslow said and got into the car. He slammed the door closed. Arthur sat up behind him and threw his head against the security screen. He shouted something at Hounslow.

With Malcolm and Alan watching from the tarmac, Hounslow stepped on the gas and sped away with lights flashing and siren wailing.

"Carl — " Malcolm began.

Judge Carl Parks wadded up a piece of paper and threw it at the trash can like a basketball. It hit the rim and bounced to the floor. "I've been robbed."

"Carl, *please*."

Carl sighed as he swiveled around in his leather chair. "He attacked the sheriff and his men, for heaven's sake." He tugged at the folds of his robe and put his feet up on his desk.

"He didn't attack them. Arguably, it was the other way around. Alan and I will testify to that," Malcolm said.

"What do you want me to do?"

"Give him bail. Put him in my custody."

The judge laughed. "Do the words *fat chance* mean anything to you?"

"Why? The hospital can't help him — and neither can time in jail. He doesn't even belong here!"

"From everything I've heard, he's exactly where he belongs," Carl declared, wadding up another piece of paper. "The psychiatric ward at the hospital is ideal."

"He's not crazy."

"He thinks he's King Arthur and he gives every indication of being a public nuisance — a *violent* public nuisance." Carl tossed the paper at the trash can. It went in. "Two points!"

"That's only because he doesn't understand what's going on. Drop yourself thirteen hundred years into the past and see how *you* cope."

Carl jabbed a finger at Malcolm. "Aha — so you *do* think he's King Arthur. I should've known. Somebody's going to lock *you* up one of these days."

Malcolm changed his approach. "Carl, listen to me. Do you pretend to understand everything there is about this world?"

"No," Carl said.

"Then you can admit that there are things beyond our comprehension."

"Yeah, sure," Carl said, a tone of boredom.

"Then use your imagination for a minute."

Carl tucked his hands behind his head. "Forget my imagination. This is reality."

"And we don't know everything there is to know about reality. That's my point!" Malcolm said.

Carl rolled his eyes heavenward. "Here it comes. The lecture."

"If necessary," Malcolm said with a nod. "You're a churchgoing man. You know that there's more to reality than what we see with our eyes, touch with our hands, experience from one second to the next. There's an *eternal* reality. A reality that slips outside the boundaries of time and space. You believe that death is just a doorway to that eternal reality, right?"

"Right, but — "

"Okay, so what if there are other kinds of doors leading to other realities — realities of different places in time — past and present all mixed up in a big house that we call eternity?"

"Malcolm — "

"And what if the many doors in that house are usually locked? But one day, the house settles a little and one of the doors cracks open and whatever was in that room slips out into the hall — into *our* time."

"Those are a lot of *what ifs*, Malcolm."

"Life is full of what ifs, Carl."

"Cut it out. If you're standing here expecting me to believe that time suddenly belched and out came King Arthur, I can't do it."

Malcolm sighed. "All right, *don't* believe it. Just administer some justice and let me take Arthur."

Carl spread his hands is surrender. "I *can't*. He's too hot right now. What'll people say if I hand down a decision letting that man loose after he assaults our police officers? Jerry Anderson is already having a field day with this in the newspaper. Releasing him will only add fuel to the fire."

"What are you suggesting?" Malcolm asked.

"Leave it alone for now," Carl said. "Let the doctors perform their tests and write up their evaluation. If he's sane, they'll say so. Then, maybe in a week or two, I'll release him to your custody. Deal?"

"A week or two! But I'm not sure we have that long."

"Why wouldn't you?" Carl asked. "Is he on some kind of schedule?"

"I'm not certain. But he's ... aging."

"Aging?"

"Yes. He's in the wrong place at the wrong time and I think it's affecting him somehow." Malcolm tried not to sound melodramatic, but spoke very seriously, "If I don't get this sorted out, the past as we know it could change."

"How?"

Malcolm didn't dare try to answer.

Carl thought about it for a moment, then shook his head. "Sorry, Malcolm. I can't let him out."

15

I II III IV V VI VII VIII IX X XI XII

Alan reached Malcolm's cottage as the sun made its final descent to the horizon. A deep red stain spread through the clouds. Weatherwise, it had been a perfect day. But Alan hadn't seen any of it. After the ambush at the airport, he'd spent the rest of the afternoon persuading Sheriff Hounslow and the doctors-in-residence to allow him into the psychiatric ward to see Arthur. "I'm the only one who can talk to him," Alan reasoned. They eventually agreed.

Alan didn't like what he saw when he had arrived in Arthur's room. The king had been heavily medicated and restrained with straps. Lines were etched deeply around his eyes, his mouth drawn, his hair a wiry gray.

Alan pulled up a chair next to the bed. Arthur signaled for him to lean closer. He whispered drowsily in Latin that he needed Alan to do something for him.

"What would be your pleasure, Majesty?" Alan asked with sincere respect.

Arthur told him.

Alan had left the hospital immediately and gone straight to Malcolm's cottage.

"Mr. Dubbs isn't here. I think he went to see the judge," Mrs. Packer said when she answered the door. "But your daughter is inside with Jeff. They're in the study."

Alan thanked her and walked to the study. She watched as he went and couldn't help but notice how his demeanor sagged as if under an invisible weight.

Jeff and Elizabeth sat on the sofa laughing at some private joke. Alan observed them silently from the doorway. They had been best of friends until their adventure in an alternative time a few months before. The trauma and near-loss they experienced took them from the love of friendship to a different kind of love. They were inseparable now. Alan didn't worry about the appropriateness of their love like many parents might. What they felt for each other seemed to transcend physical preoccupations. There would be no premature wedding night. Jeff and Elizabeth had made that perfectly clear.

"Daddy?" Elizabeth had looked up to face her father. "We were waiting for you. Is everything all right?"

"Hi," he said with a fake smile. He slumped down into the chair next to them.

"What's wrong, Mr. Forde?" Jeff asked.

He washed a hand over his face. "I'm a little tired."

"We heard what happened at the airport. How's King Arthur?" Elizabeth asked anxiously.

"Not very well, I'm afraid to say." Alan breathed deeply. "God help the poor man. It's bad enough being thrown into the future, but to get handcuffed and thrown into a psychiatric ward ..." Alan shivered involuntarily.

"You look pale, Daddy. Maybe you should rest for a while," Elizabeth suggested.

"I can't. Arthur asked me to do something for him."

"What?" Elizabeth asked.

"He wants his sword and clothes taken back to the church ruin," Alan explained wearily. "He said it's where they belong. They're not safe anywhere else. He's afraid of what might happen if Excalibur falls into the wrong hands."

Jeff was on his feet instantly. "I can do it."

"We can do it," Elizabeth corrected him.

Alan nodded his approval, relieved to have someone else share his burden. "Here's what you have to do ..."

○ ○ ○

They reverently placed Arthur's carefully cleaned and folded clothes (compliments of Mrs. Packer) in the backseat of Jeff's Volkswagen Bug. Because of its length, the sword had to be angled in to fit.

"Be careful," Alan said as they pulled away amidst the loud sputter and pop of Jeff's car.

"Why do you think he told us to be careful?" Jeff asked, wondering if there was a potential danger he wasn't aware of.

Elizabeth shrugged. "That was just Dad being Dad. He's been like that ever since we got back." *We got back* was the phrase they used to refer to their time travel without actually talking about it.

Things had changed at the church ruin since they were last there. Outside, a large truck was parked next to the barricade entrance, obviously leftover by the construction workers who'd been busy throughout the day. Inside, new scaffolding had been built along two of the walls. Jeff lugged the sword like he would a pair of skis on his shoulder. Elizabeth carried the clothes and a large flashlight.

"I don't like this," Elizabeth said in response to the dancing shadows and the eerie crypt-like appearance of the church.

"I just hope they didn't move the stone table," Jeff said.

Elizabeth dodged one of the pillars and moved the flashlight around like a spotlight. "There it is," she pointed. It was half-hidden on the other side of a pallet of drywall.

They approached the stone tablet and stared at it silently for a moment. Jeff felt a strong urge to pray, but was afraid that Elizabeth might think he was being overdramatic.

"It looks like a coffin." Elizabeth shivered.

"Quit scaring yourself," Jeff said.

"What did King Arthur want us to do?" Elizabeth asked.

Jeff moved around to the side of the table. "According to your father, we need to move the top to one side. It's like a big, hollow stone box on the inside, I guess. Then we're supposed to hide his stuff inside."

"Then what?"

"That's all."

"But what if one of these construction workers finds it?" asked Elizabeth.

"I wasn't the one who talked to Arthur about it," said Jeff. "Your dad said specifically to put everything in here."

"But *why*?"

"I don't know," Jeff answered. "Maybe he figures that, since this was where he came into our time, it's the same way out."

"I don't like it," Elizabeth said.

"You'll get over it," Jeff said with a grin.

He leaned against the lid of the table and pushed. It didn't move. "It's heavy, that's for sure," he said and pushed again.

Elizabeth positioned the flashlight on the pallet, then wrapped her hands claw-like over the edge and pulled from the other side. The top jerked loose with a loud scrape, then slid slowly to one side.

"That's enough," Jeff gasped as he collapsed against the flat stone. He wiped away the beads of sweat on his brow with the back of his hand.

Elizabeth bent down and retrieved the bundle of clothes. She placed them inside the table then shivered. "It gives me the creeps," she said.

"I know, I know," Jeff said with a nod. With a grunt, he picked up Excalibur and slid it into the table next to the clothes. Again, they both fell silent. Jeff looked across the table at Elizabeth.

Her eyes were fixed on the dark hole inside the box.

"Bits?" Jeff asked. He didn't like the vacant expression that had passed over her face.

She tilted her head to the left.

"Bits," Jeff called out. "I think we better get out of here." He pulled on the stone lid.

"Vale: oremus semper," she said softly.

Jeff stopped and looked at her wide-eyed. "What did you say?"

Startled, Elizabeth put her hand to her mouth and looked at him. "Huh?"

"What did you just say?"

She looked stricken. "I don't know. That was so weird."

"It sounded like you said something in Latin!" he said.

"Did I?" Elizabeth asked nervously. She wrapped her arms around herself. "Hurry up, Jeff. I don't want to stay here. It's scaring me."

"Okay. Help me," Jeff said. He and Elizabeth pushed the lid back into place. Certain that it was secure, they headed for the doorway.

At the doorway out, they both stopped and turned to look back at the table.

"Do you hear that?" Jeff asked.

"Yes."

It was a low hum, pulsating. A fog seemed to appear from nowhere and now swirled at their feet. A green and yellow light seemed to glow from *inside* the stone table. It glowed through the sides and top as if the box was made of glass instead of stone. Jeff blinked and Elizabeth rubbed her arms.

"The clothes — the sword!" Elizabeth said.

"I see them," Jeff assured her. They could now see the clothes and the sword *through* the thick stone of the table.

The light grew brighter and brighter until it was a blinding, brilliant white.

"Turn away!" Jeff called out as he put his hands up to protect

Elizabeth. Elizabeth covered her face and caught the scream that rose in her throat.

Then the light suddenly went out, the hum faded, and even the fog raced away in patches like white mice to the corners of the church.

Jeff grabbed the flashlight from Elizabeth and rushed to the stone table. With all the adrenaline now surging through his body, he pushed on the lid with all his might. It moved more easily this time. He shone the beam of the flashlight into the dark box.

"Jeff, what was that? What happened?"

Jeff looked up at Elizabeth. "It's empty. The sword and the clothes are gone."

16

I II III IV V VI VII VIII IX X XI XII

"Well, now, look at you." Ponsonby smiled graciously as he walked into the garage.

Adrian was in the middle of polishing the Rolls Royce. He'd been working for Ponsonby almost a week and, as yet, hadn't driven any of the cars. His job initially was to polish the exteriors of the cars and treat the leather interiors. Simple mechanical work — changing the oil, brake fluids, and the like — was also his to do. Anything more complicated was left to experts. Apparently driving the cars would be left to experts too. Adrian was disappointed about that. But the pay was surprisingly generous and Adrian figured that, if nothing else, he could work a few weeks and use the money to take a nice, long trip for the rest of the summer.

"Lewis tells me you're doing excellent work," Ponsonby said, referring to the supervisor of the garage. He walked back and forth along the fronts of the cars like a general inspecting a formation of men. "From the looks of the cars, I agree."

"Thank you, Mr. Ponsonby," Adrian said proudly.

Ponsonby had shown a keen interest in Adrian during the course of the week. At various points in the day he arrived at the garage with a tray of tea and sat to chat with Adrian. All subjects were fair game. He asked Adrian about his childhood, his interests, his hopes and dreams. Interspersed with the questions were Ponsonby's observations and philosophies about life. "If you let it, all the baggage of your childhood can cripple you for life," Ponsonby had said. "A slight on the schoolyard, a bully who wouldn't leave you alone, hurt feelings and lost love ... they can come back to haunt you as an adult and impair your ability to make sensible decisions. Suddenly you're cowering in front of your competitors like you did that bully. Suddenly you're resentful of allies because you remember the ones who hurt your feelings when you were a child. But once you realize you have the baggage, you can get rid of it. You can overcome the past to conquer your future."

Adrian was getting a crash course in Ponsonby Maxims. He didn't mind, though. Ponsonby made good sense. His ideas and comments triggered feelings in Adrian, making him feel like things *were* possible, fortunes could be attained, dreams could be made realities. You simply had to have the inner resources to do it. *I really am the master of my fate*, Adrian thought.

What a contrast to his own father. The two men were complete opposites. Where Ponsonby was charismatic and aggressive, Adrian's father was gentle and sensitive. Where Ponsonby made hard decisions that usually turned out to be correct, Adrian's father waffled on most decisions that were often wrong, even though he'd thought them through to the *n*th degree. The truth was, Adrian loved his father but he began to feel he'd rather be like Ponsonby. The realization made him feel guilty.

"Montagu, my valet, has a mother who's gone in hospital in York," Ponsonby said. "I'd like you to fill in for him while he's away. It may only be a week or so."

Adrian stopped polishing the car. "Me? Be your valet?"

"Yes."

"But I've never been a valet before," Adrian said. "I don't know the first thing about it."

"Are you telling me you can't learn or are you saying that you don't want to do it?" Ponsonby asked with that challenging look in his eyes.

"Of course, I *want* to do it, but — "

"If you *want to*, then you'll learn quickly. If I were worried about your ability, I wouldn't have asked. I'm asking because I have every confidence in you. A valet is nothing more than a personal assistant," Ponsonby asserted. "There'll be extra pay, of course. Will you do it?"

"Yes, sir."

"Excellent. I'll have Lewis go home with you to get your things."

Adrian was confused. "Get my things?"

"Yes," Ponsonby said. "If you're going to be my valet, you'll have to move in."

✹ ✹ ✹

"So your Arthur character is crazy as a loon. He attacked some policemen and they put him in a mental ward," Graham said, referring to the small article he'd found on the Internet and printed out.

Myrddin fingered the page. "Not necessarily. Just because they locked him up doesn't mean they're right."

"Well, if Arthur's come back to make a good impression, he's started off on the wrong footing," said Graham.

"I don't believe Arthur has come back to make a good impression," Myrddin said earnestly.

"Then why did he — I mean, hypothetically speaking, *if* such a thing was remotely possible — why *would* he come back?" Graham asked.

"He would come back to make things right."

"Cure social ills? Start a charity?" Graham inquired. His tone was glib.

"Perhaps."

Graham pressed on. "What are you saying, that he'll come back to be our king again? Don't you think our current monarch might be a bit cheesed off at the intrusion? I can see the two of them now, battling over who'll attend the opening of the new shopping centre, or christening the ship or whatever it is our monarchs do these days."

Myrddin pointed a warning finger at him. "Don't be disrespectful."

"Then what do you think Arthur will do?" Graham asked. "Lead England to newfound victory somewhere? Restore the glory of Camelot? Wave Excalibur around a few times and bring back the Empire?"

Myrddin shook his head. "You're thinking in very obvious terms, Graham. What is England's greatest need?"

Graham thought for a moment. "Most would say it's the economy. Will he come back to become the Chancellor of the Exchequer?"

"No." Myrddin sighed. "I thought that you, of all people, would know the answer."

Graham frowned, suddenly feeling as if he'd failed a test he didn't even known he was taking. "Sorry. I don't think there *is* an answer because Arthur isn't coming back. It's a fantasy, Myrddin, a myth."

"Not all myths are untrue, Graham," Myrddin declared.

"Perhaps not," he responded harshly. "But I don't have time for myths, true or untrue. I have reality to deal with. I have a collapsing church, a struggling parish, a wayward son. Indulge in the legends of King Arthur if you want to, but don't expect me to stop my life to play along."

Myrddin didn't say anything. The two men stared at one another.

Graham blushed. "I'm sorry, Myrddin. I don't know where that came from."

"It came from your heart," Myrddin said softly.

"Yes, it did. That's what scares me."

"Go home, Graham," Myrddin said with a wave of his hand, but not in an unkind tone. "Go home to your realities."

○ ○ ○

Adrian had just finished putting a suitcase into the back of Lewis's car when Graham arrived. He glanced at his father as the Mini pulled to a stop, then went back into the house.

Graham got out of his car and walked to the driver's side of the beige Land Rover. "Hello, Lewis," Graham said to the leprechaun-like face just inside the window, which currently had a cigarette dangling from its lips.

"'lo, Reverend." Lewis nodded, the cigarette flicked.

"So ... what's all this then?"

"Adrian's moving in with Ponsonby," Anne said. She was leaning against the kitchen doorway with her arms folded. "I've already talked to him. There's nothing we can do."

"What do you mean there's nothing we can do? We're his parents. Adrian!" he called out.

"Hello, Dad," Adrian said casually as he slipped past his mother in the doorway. He was carrying an armload of books to the car.

"Your mother tells me you're moving out — and moving in with Ponsonby."

"Not permanently. He needs me for a couple of weeks," Adrian replied and tossed the books in the back. He closed the lid.

"You could've asked first."

"Why? Would you have said yes?"

"We might have after some consideration," Graham said.

"I didn't have a month for you to work out your considerations," Adrian said sharply. "Ponsonby needed to know right away."

"He doesn't have a phone?"

"Is there something wrong, Dad? It's a straightforward job. It pays well. You won't miss me. You can pretend I'm away at school again."

"That's not what I'm talking about," Graham said and took Adrian by the arm to lead him away from the car and Lewis. "You know how I feel about your working for Ponsonby at all. He's an unscrupulous man. He spins little webs and you could easily get caught up in one. He'll pull you in, influence you. Let's be honest about this. He stands for everything we're against — or should I say that he's against everything we stand for."

"And what's that, Dad? What do you stand for? The old church? The archdeacon?"

"Adrian!" Anne snapped from the doorway.

"I'm just asking, since we're being honest. You talk about standing for something and I don't know what it is. I don't see it. At least you know with Mr. Ponsonby. He doesn't sit around wringing his hands about things that don't matter. He *does* something. He's *doing* something with his life. Maybe he'll help me do something with mine."

Graham was speechless.

Anne strode toward Adrian from the doorway, crossing the gap in only a few long steps. "What are you implying?"

Adrian looked away.

"You apologize to your father!" Anne commanded.

"It's all right, darling," Graham said quietly. "He was only speaking his heart. Go to Ponsonby if that's what you want." Graham walked into the house.

Anne was aghast. "You can go," she said, turning angrily to her son. "But I'm not sure you should come back until you learn to *respect* your father. He's a good man and what you said was … was …" The rest of the sentence never came. The words were choked off by angry tears. She spun around and marched into the house, making sure to slam the door behind her.

Adrian grimaced and went to the car.

17

I II III IV V VI VII VIII IX X XI XII

"A perfect cup of tea. Thank you, Mrs. Packer," Colin Jenkins said happily.

Mrs. Packer nodded. "You're welcome," she said and whisked out of the room.

Malcolm sipped his tea. "I appreciate you driving all this way, Colin. You didn't have to do it. I could've flown down again."

"I needed time away from the city anyway," Colin said. "It's lovely country you have in this part of the state. Besides, I wanted to deliver this personally." He handed over a small brown envelope. "It's for your friend."

Malcolm took the envelope and opened it up. Inside was a passport. Malcolm pulled it out and perused the inside. It had a photo of Arthur — taken the day they were at the British Embassy — and the name Arthur Pendragon, complete with appropriate biographical and administrative details to give him safe passage into England. "Colin," Malcolm began to say, appreciatively.

"You know that you must only use it this one time, then destroy it," Colin cautioned him.

"Uh huh," Malcolm answered. He wasn't a novice when it came to this sort of work. He flipped through the pages. Some bore the Immigration stamps of England, Canada, the United States, and Australia.

Malcolm struggled with his conscience, then said, "Look, Colin, I know you think you're helping me with an Intelligence matter, but you're not. We're not on the kind of mission you think. I tried to tell you at the Embassy but ..." Malcolm was at a loss for words. "I'm sorry."

Colin smiled uncomfortably. "Then what's this all about?"

Malcolm took a deep breath and decided, for better or worse, to tell him everything. "Mrs. Packer," he called out. "I think you'd better bring a fresh pot of tea."

⚙ ⚙ ⚙

Alan was worried. Arthur looked at least twenty years older than he'd been when he first arrived in Fawlt Line. His strength and vibrancy had dimmed to a near-feeble state. He barely spoke and, when he did, it was in a hoarse whisper. The doctors didn't bother to restrain his arms anymore. He lay in his hospital bed like any other mentally ill geriatric patient.

Alan wished Malcolm was allowed in to see him, to impress upon him the urgency of the situation. But Malcolm couldn't get in. Sheriff Hounslow had left strict instructions that Alan Forde was the only one permitted to see the patient.

"Can't you release him now?" Alan asked Dr. Carey, the supervisor of the Psychiatric Ward.

"No," Dr. Carey answered directly. His lean face reminded Alan of a greyhound. "Our tests aren't completed. We're dealing with an extremely advanced form of dementia."

"But can't you see what being here is doing to him?"

"This is a hospital, Mr. Forde. If he's ill, this is the best place for him to be." Dr. Carey smirked.

Alan restrained all he wanted to say to that smirk and went back to Arthur's room. Malcolm knew what was at stake, Alan reasoned. If there's any way to get Arthur out of this hospital, he'll try it.

"How do you feel, your Majesty?" Alan asked in Latin.

"I am plagued by dreams," Arthur answered. "I see my kingdom crumbling beneath the treachery of Mordred."

Alan remembered how both Arthur and Mordred killed each other in that last decisive battle and Camelot went the way of all dreams. He bit his lip. What would happen to history if Arthur died here and now in present day Fawlt Line?

Alan changed the subject. "Much has been written about the Holy Grail, my Lord. Would you be gracious enough to tell me from your own point of view what really happened?"

At the mention of the Grail, Arthur's expression lit up. "The Grail belonged to Joseph of Arimathea, my ancestor and the first bishop of Christianity in England, who brought my country to the knowledge of the salvation of our Lord Jesus Christ. It was the dish used by our Lord himself at the final feast with his disciples, before his betrayal, crucifixion and, thanks be to God, his resurrection. Alas, it was never seen by me. I cannot tell you from whence it came or whither it went, though we knew it was hidden within our shores."

"Why did you send your knights to find it?"

"As Merlin had prophesied years before, my kingdom became plagued by great evil, my barons fighting against each other for land, knights killing one another for mere sport; murder and thievery abounded. Some even forsook Christ himself and turned to an evil faith and cruel worship of the pagan gods of Britain. These evils threatened to tear the kingdom to pieces. So I beseeched my kinsman, the archbishop, 'Tell me how to rid my country of evil.' He spoke unto me and said that the Grail must be found, for with the Grail would come healing upon my land."

"Is that when you created the Knights of the Round Table?"

"Indeed! They rode from Camelot with great fanfare. Yet I was heavy of heart for I knew that many would never return. For two years my knights searched the land for the Grail, battling evil where they found it. Many died as I had feared, whilst others became sick at heart and gave up the quest. It came about that

Sir Galahad, Sir Perceval, and Sir Bors encountered one another in their travels and determined to ride together to find the Grail. They performed many marvelous deeds and in time united many of the barons of the Northern Lands against the pagans. That is, until they saw the vision."

"What vision?" Alan asked.

"I will not tell the entire story. In Scotland, they had rescued the Earl Hernox from captivity at the hands of cruel pagan knights. After their great victory, they were assembled in a room in the castle. Suddenly, the doors slammed shut, all went dark, and a loud, rushing wind arose as if making a mournful cry. Though terrified, my knights fled not. Then a bright light filled the room, so dazzling that it was pain to look upon, yet my knights could not help themselves, for through the light they saw a beautifully laid table. Upon the table was a wide dish of silver. Then the doors opened and an old man, dressed as a bishop, appeared at the side of the table. On the breast of his robe were written the words *Joseph, Who Did Take Our Lord's Body From the Cross*."

"It was an apparition of Joseph of Arimathea!" Alan exclaimed.

Arthur nodded. "My knights were sore vexed, but remained where they were. Seeing their consternation, the bishop smiled upon them and said, 'Marvel not, good knights, for though I am but a spirit, I have come to help thee.' The bishop bade them eat from the silver dish upon the table and it was the sweetest, most marvelous food they had eaten in all of their lives. After which, the bishop asked them if they knew what the vessel was from which they had eaten. The knights said they knew not. The bishop told them that it was the holy vessel out of which our Lord ate before he was betrayed and killed on the cross. He redeemed the world if men would but choose his way."

"The Holy Grail itself," said Alan.

"So it was," Arthur continued. "The bishop, who had spoken unto them in a surpassing sweet and pleasant manner, suddenly spoke sadly. 'So you shall see it. But none other of your kind will ever see it. On this night it will depart from your land.' The three knights wept grievously for without the Grail, they knew their king and country were lost. Good Sir Galahad asked if there was nothing they could do to keep the Grail and turn the land from its wicked ways. The bishop said sorrowfully that there was not. 'Have you not tried for two years to rid the land of its evil? Were not your labors and battling in vain? No, it is the will of God that this land and its people shall be abandoned to their own evil devices. Sorrow, death, treachery, and rebellion will come at the hands of those who live to seek only fortune and profit. The pagans will attempt to blot out the very memory of God and Christ. The sanctuaries of prayers will become lairs of wolves. Owls will nest where hymns of praise were sung. Doom and desolation will fill the hearts of all, for there will be no godly comfort to aid them.'"

"You have just described our modern world," Alan said sadly.

Arthur went on with his story. "The bishop turned to Galahad and Perceval and said that inasmuch as they were pure and unspotted from evil, their souls would go with him when he departed. He then looked upon Sir Bors and said that he would live to fight for Christ yet awhile longer and to tell the king all he had seen and heard. Suddenly a blinding light filled the room and Sir Bors fell backward from the table, the bishop, and his two friends. After a time, the light faded and Sir Bors saw Galahad and Perceval on their knees where the table had been. But, going to the two knights, he discerned that the spirit had departed from them. They fell over dead. Sir Bors, with a sorrowful heart, returned to Camelot and told me all that had happened. I and my remaining knights wept openly for the loss of the age and the terror that would one day come." A tear slid down Arthur's cheek. "I still fight for the good, Alan, and for the glory of Camelot, but evil presses in and I am weary. God grant that this dream would end now, for I am heavy of heart."

Alan sat speechless, wanting to say something to comfort the king, but unable to find the words. Suddenly the door was flung open by a pale-faced Officer Massey, who had been assigned to keep guard at Arthur's door. A middle-aged man in a dark suit and jet black sunglasses strode into the room. It was Colin Jenkins.

"What's going on?" Alan asked.

"This is the man," Jenkins announced to Officer Massey.

Dr. Carey, who followed hot on his heels, stammered, "But you can't just *take* him."

Colin turned on him. "Is it normally your policy to argue with the British Secret Service? Must I show you my badge again?"

"No, of course not," Carey blubbered, "but don't you need some kind of warrant or subpoena or ... or official paperwork?"

Colin leaned toward him, his jaw set so tight that Alan could see the muscles working. "Oh, you'll get paperwork all right. The lot of you may be indicted for harboring this fugitive. Can he walk?"

"Yes," Carey said. "We think so."

Colin pointed to Alan. "I understand you're his translator. Help me take him out."

Confused, Alan whispered to Arthur that they were leaving and helped him to his feet.

"Maybe I should call the sheriff," Officer Massey offered.

"And put it out all over your radio waves that I'm here? Are you mad?" Colin cried out. "Are you trying to cause an international incident?"

"No, sir," Officer Massey retreated.

"Get his clothes," Colin said to Alan. Alan nodded, rushed to the wardrobe, and grabbed what he could. "We'll have him change in the car. Time is of the essence."

"I'd still like to make a call," Dr. Carey said nervously.

"If you're willing to risk a national emergency, fine, call whomever you like *five minutes after we leave*," Colin barked.

Carey agreed.

With Arthur between them, Colin and Alan went down the hall, through the security door, and to the rear stairwell. Colin's car was parked at the back door. They helped Arthur into the back seat. Alan got in the passenger side and Colin pointed a threatening finger at Dr. Carey, who was fluttering nearby. "If you love your country, then I wasn't here. You never saw me."

Dr. Carey nodded his head vigorously.

Colin got into the car, started it up, and pulled away with a dramatic screech of his tires against the pavement.

"What in the world is going on?" Alan asked, once they'd cleared the hospital grounds and were well on their way out of Fawlt Line.

Colin exhaled and his whole tough-guy demeanor evaporated. "I'm going to lose my job, *that's* what's going on."

"But . . . where are you taking us?"

"To the airport. You have a plane to catch."

✿ ✿ ✿

"The *British* Secret Service?" Hounslow bellowed. The veins in his neck stood out and a throbbing pulse was visible on his forehead. "Did you get the agent's name?"

"Not really. He flashed his badge and . . . it happened so fast," Officer Massey replied.

Hounslow scrubbed his face and let his fingers run through his thinning hair. "Malcolm's behind this. I just know it."

"How could I know?" Massey asked, defensively.

"You don't have enough brain cells to know," Hounslow said, then muttered to himself, "They probably went to the airport. They'll take Malcolm's plane."

"Should we go after them?" Massey asked.

Hounslow sighed. "No. They're long gone by now."

"We could call the air controller — "

"Let them go," Hounslow interrupted. "Good riddance to that maniac."

"Whatever you say," Massey said, and slinked out of the office.

Hounslow hit his fist against the desktop. It wasn't losing Arthur. It wasn't even the ridiculous British Secret Service scam. More than anything, he *hated* Malcolm Dubbs for getting one up on him again.

At the small Fawlt Line airport, Malcolm got Alan, Jeff, and Arthur onto his plane. The plan was to fly to Dulles Airport where they would catch the next commercial flight to London. Malcolm walked over to Colin, who stood next to his car at the edge of the tarmac.

"Thank you, Colin. You have no idea what — "

"I don't want to know," Colin said with a hint of a smile. "If anyone ever says I was involved in this lunacy, I'll deny it."

"Right."

"You'll burn his passport when you get to England."

"Understood."

Colin grabbed Malcolm's hand and shook it. "Call me when you get back. Perhaps we can go out for a *normal* dinner?"

"Certainly."

"Provided we're not in jail," he said before he got into his car and drove off.

Malcolm boarded his plane and taxied out for the takeoff. "Everybody ready?"

A chorus of assent came back to him from the cabin.

"Then it's off to that green and pleasant land," Malcolm said and revved the engines.

Arthur didn't panic this time.

There was a problem with a passport, but not Arthur's. Alan didn't realize until they arrived at Dulles Airport that his passport had expired only three weeks before.

In the wild rush to get to the plane, quick good-byes were all they could manage. Malcolm felt terrible that poor Alan, after working so hard, wouldn't get to see the end of the story — whatever that end might be. Alan calmly smiled and then explained to Arthur that he wouldn't be going with them.

Arthur was indignant. His face reflected his desire to throw a royal fit; to demand that Alan be allowed on the plane. But he was still weakened and didn't try. He suddenly embraced Alan. "If I had Excalibur, I would knight you. You are as courageous and true as the best of my knights. God grant I may return and do this very good thing for you," he said in Latin.

"Thank you, your Highness. God be with you."

Alan stood alone as Malcolm, Jeff, and Arthur walked through the security check for international flights. Arthur looked back at him one last time.

18

I II III IV V VI VII VIII IX X XI XII

At 6:30 in the morning, the Boeing Triple–7 bumped gently as it landed on the airstrip at London's Heathrow airport. Arthur watched sleepily from his window seat as they taxied through an early morning fog toward the terminal. He breathed in deeply as if he might take in some English air, then put his head back and closed his eyes again.

From the seat across the aisle, Malcolm wondered what was going through Arthur's mind. Without Alan, there was no way to communicate directly with him apart from the obvious hand gestures. Malcolm could've kicked himself for not studying Latin in college as he'd planned. The cabin crew was sympathetic to the gray-haired old man who didn't speak English and didn't eat with utensils. It was unspoken among them that he was probably senile.

The plane pulled up to the gate and Malcolm felt the butterflies stir to life in his stomach. Along with the rest of the passengers, he, Jeff, and Arthur walked the endless halls and moving walkways to Passport Control. It was an enormous room filled with travelers from all over the world, herded into several lines to accommodate their many different categories.

Malcolm gestured to Jeff. "You go through the visitor's line. I'll escort Arthur through the residents' line. And let's hope nothing happens."

Their line moved quickly and Malcolm and Arthur were directed to a Passport Control desk. The clerk took their passports and Malcolm explained that his friend didn't speak English very well, so he was traveling with him. The clerk double-checked the photos, flipped through the pages of their passports, stamped them, then waved them through. They stepped through to the other side of the podium and Malcolm breathed a sigh of relief.

The visitor's line had more people in it, so it took Jeff longer to reach a Passport Control podium. Malcolm watched as the clerk asked Jeff a few questions. Then Jeff, looking flustered, checked his pockets and, spying Malcolm, waved him over. "He wants to see my return ticket," he called.

"Oh," Malcolm said, feeling foolish for not giving it to Jeff in the first place. He gave Arthur a "Wait here" gesture and walked over to Jeff and the passport clerk. He handed over Jeff's ticket, keeping a watch on Arthur from the corner of his eye.

The clerk was satisfied, stamped Jeff's passport, and allowed him through. Malcolm and Jeff turned to Arthur, and were startled to see him talking to a man in a rumpled suit.

"What's this?" Malcolm exclaimed loud enough for a couple of people around him to turn to look.

Arthur, looking confused, took a few steps away from the man. The man followed and said something else to Arthur. Arthur looked at Malcolm helplessly then turned on the man, shouting something at him in Latin and walking away toward Malcolm. The man backed off for a moment then followed Arthur.

"It'll only take a minute," the man was saying to Arthur as he approached Malcolm and Jeff.

"Excuse me. Can I help you with something?" Malcolm asked with a strained friendliness.

"You're with this gentleman," the man said. "I was behind you in the queue."

"Yes — and is there something wrong?" Malcolm asked.

"Not at all." The man fished around in his jacket pocket and produced a small billfold, flipping, it open to reveal journalism credentials for a newspaper called *The London Post*. His name was Andy Samuelson. "Fair enough?"

"What do you want?" Malcolm asked, even less friendly now that he knew he was talking to a newspaperman and not an Immigration official.

"I've just flown in from America, like you. I was on assignment," the reporter said.

"So?"

Samuelson pushed a lock of his straight black hair away from his eyes. "I overheard the clerk say your friend's name is Arthur Pendragon. So I thought, Arthur *Pendragon* — as in *King* Arthur? — and I was curious. Anything's got potential for a story, if you know what I mean. So I asked him to tell me about himself."

"Did he?" Malcolm asked.

"Was he putting me on or was that Latin he shouted at me?"

"It was," Malcolm said. "But we're not interested in doing any interviews."

"What are you, his agent?"

"We're friends who've had a very long flight. Now, if you'll excuse us — " Malcolm signaled for Arthur and Jeff to follow him as he brushed past the reporter.

Samuelson followed them. "Tell me one thing: is that his real name or is it made up? Is he a descendant of Arthur?"

"You asked *two* things. We really don't have time," Malcolm said over his shoulder. They got onto the escalator that took them down to the baggage claim.

"Why won't you talk to me? It'd be a wonderful human interest story. He even *looks* like what I imagined Arthur to look like. Perhaps a bit older," Samuelson said from a few stairs above them on the escalator.

Malcolm turned to him. "Please leave us alone or I'll get airport security."

"Suit yourself," Samuelson said, and strolled away from them once they reached the bottom of the escalator.

Jeff looked thoughtful as they walked to the baggage carousel. "Malcolm ... why not talk to that reporter? Maybe that'll help with Arthur's mission. I mean, shouldn't he meet up with the queen or the prime minister or somebody in charge?"

"Oh, you've figured out what his mission is? You *know* that's what he should do?" Malcolm asked.

"No, but — "

"Jeff, until we have some clear leading, I don't want anyone to know who he is. I can't imagine anything more distracting than a media circus around him."

"Okay, okay," Jeff said defensively. "So what do we do now?"

"You get our luggage and go through customs while I get the rental car," Malcolm said. "I'll meet you by the curb out front."

"Then what?"

"We'll go to the hotel — and the hope that something will happen to help us know whatever we're supposed to do."

"You mean, like a phone call or a message left in our room?" Jeff said, smiling.

"Don't be cheeky," Malcolm said and walked toward the exit through customs.

Jeff looked over at Arthur, who stood erect, his arms folded across his chest and his eyes fixed on the baggage coming down the ramp to the moving carousel. Jeff blinked and looked again. Maybe it was Jeff's imagination, but Arthur seemed to look *younger.*

⚙ ⚙ ⚙

Jeff and Arthur cleared customs without incident and made their way to the curb in front of the terminal. Nothing in the roar of the traffic or the concrete parking garage straight ahead gave Jeff the impression that England was much different from America.

He looked over at Arthur, who looked back and forth with an expression of incredulity. Just then a large double-decker bus drove past, belching black fumes. Arthur coughed violently and said something in Latin that sounded abusive.

"We have to wait for Malcolm," Jeff tried to say through words and gestures.

Arthur tilted his head slowly as if to acknowledge that he knew what Jeff had said. He leaned against the terminal wall and put his hands in his pockets.

He could be any business traveler, Jeff thought. Even the disheveled hair and beard gave him the look of an eccentric. And there was no mistaking it now in the morning light. Jeff was certain: Arthur looked better, healthier.

Arthur was invigorated, that much he knew. The smells emitting from the machines offended him, and the absence of green land alarmed him, but he felt better here. Somehow, he knew he was home. Perhaps it was magic.

"This, then, is my Britain?" Arthur asked Jeff in Latin, to confirm it.

Jeff indicated that he didn't understand.

"It is my desire to see the land," Arthur said, growing impatient.

Jeff smiled vacantly, not understanding.

Arthur's eye caught sight of a bus as it pulled to a stop two lanes away. It was large, with an upstairs and downstairs, and was painted to look like a green field. *That is my land*, Arthur thought.

Twenty feet away from Jeff, the automatic doors of the terminal whisked open and Andy Samuelson stepped out onto the pavement. He frowned at the daylight and popped a piece of breath-freshening gum into his mouth.

Oh no, Jeff thought as Samuelson saw him and came in his direction. Jeff tried to think of a way to escape.

Just then, Samuelson looked beyond Jeff and called, "Is he supposed to do that?"

Jeff frowned at Samuelson. A horn blared. Jeff turned around in time to see Arthur crossing the road with a complete disregard of the traffic.

"Your Highness!" Jeff cried out and raced after him.

With a screech, a car skidded to a halt in front of Jeff and nearly knocked him over. Jeff apologized quickly at the swearing driver and moved on toward Arthur, who was headed for a large, green double-decker bus sitting at the curb. Jeff was horrified to see Arthur step onto it.

"No!" Jeff shouted, and stumbled for the bus. He plowed through the waiting crowd of people and narrowly missed colliding with a woman pushing a baby in a stroller. "Wait!" he yelled.

The driver was just about to pull the bus door closed when Jeff leapt on.

"Is the big bloke with you?" the driver asked.

"Yeah," Jeff answered breathlessly, searching with his eyes the rows of seats.

"Then that'll be thirty quid," the driver said.

"What?"

The driver snorted impatiently. "Thirty *pounds*."

Confused, Jeff said, "But I don't belong on this bus."

"Obviously your friend thinks you do. C'mon, mate, we're on a tight schedule. It's not called the London-Bristol *Express* for nothing," he said. "Thirty pounds."

Jeff reached into his pocket and pulled out some money, thankful Malcolm had given him some before they left. He carefully picked away at the strange bills and handed it over. Seeing Arthur toward the back of the bus, he headed down the aisle. Arthur was smiling contentedly.

"What are you doing?" Jeff asked. "We shouldn't be on this bus."

Jeff nearly lost his footing as the bus pulled away from the curb.

"Hold it," Jeff said. He turned to tell the driver to stop, but Arthur suddenly grabbed his arm and pulled him into the seat. "What are — ?"

He shook a finger at Jeff as if to say, "No."

"I've never been in England before. We don't know where we're going. What about Malcolm?" he asked.

Arthur patted Jeff's arm.

Jeff sunk into the seat. *Malcolm isn't going to be happy about this.*

✿ ✿ ✿

Malcolm pulled his white rental car to the curb and searched the pockets of people for Jeff and Arthur. He didn't see them. As he climbed out of the car, aware that the security guards would yell at him to move, he spied Andy Samuelson leaning against the wall. The reporter had a smug look on his face — and he pointed toward the luggage at his feet. It was Malcolm's luggage.

"What's going on?" Malcolm asked.

"I've been keeping the police from confiscating your bags," he said. "They tend to assume that unaccompanied luggage contains bombs."

"Where are Jeff and Arthur?"

Samuelson grinned. "I hope you have a sense of humor."

That same morning, Adrian knocked on Ponsonby's study door, then slipped inside. "You wanted to see me, sir?"

Ponsonby was standing at his desk with a man Adrian didn't know. "Ah, Adrian, just the man we need for this meeting. Come in." The desk was covered with large sheets of paper of different sizes and colors. As Adrian got closer, he saw that they were maps; topographical maps, survey maps, and maps with notations written all over them.

"Do you know Mr. Clydesdale?" Ponsonby asked without waiting for an answer. "He is our liaison, if you will, with the various town councils. We've been strategizing about new sites for my superstores. Come look at these maps of the area."

Rounding the desk, Adrian looked down at the maps and wondered why he felt like he was about to take an exam.

"Now, here're our choices. See if *you* can choose a site for one of our superstores," he said.

Adrian was right. It was a test. And, to his surprise, he cared deeply about not wanting to fail it.

Ponsonby rifled through the maps, then pointed to an area on one. "We thought of *this* area. The farmers are actually quite keen to give it up. But it's a run-off area that gets awfully soggy if it rains too much."

Adrian wanted to say something profound, but didn't want to

sound like he was showing off. He went for the most obvious. "I think you'd have drainage problems."

Ponsonby smiled as he gestured to another map. "This area here is certainly agreeable, but it's remote."

"You would have to spend a small fortune to get a road to it, I suppose," Adrian offered.

"Exactly," Ponsonby said, then turned to another map. "This one is perfect but we've been warned that some kind of rare species of hedgehog lives there."

Adrian rubbed his chin. This wasn't as hard as he thought. "You'll battle environmental and animal rights groups every step of the way."

Ponsonby shot a knowing look at Mr. Clydesdale. "Didn't I tell you he has good instincts?" Ponsonby tossed a couple of maps aside, then rested his hand on another. It was a surveyor's map with numbers and codes scribbled all over it, but no identifying markings that Adrian recognized. "This one is the most promising. It is an area with two intersecting major roads, an ideal topography, and several major towns and cities within a twenty-mile radius. There's a problem, however."

"Sir?"

"The site has an old building, of no significant historical value, but an old building nonetheless. There's a stubborn tenant, a traditionalist, who believes the building should be safeguarded, even at the expense of progress."

Ponsonby paused and Adrian knew he was supposed to make an observation or ask an intelligent question. "Does the tenant actually own the building or does it belong to someone else?"

"An excellent question," Ponsonby commended him. "He doesn't own it, but he is essentially the authority over it by virtue of his job. He's responsible and his employers recognize his authority. Unless, of course, something happens to diminish his standing with them, or extenuating circumstances cause his removal."

"You've spoken to him? He understands how a superstore will help the local economy?" Adrian's voice was not his own. The question was unlike any he thought he was capable of asking.

"I have," Ponsonby replied. "The tenant is simply unreasonable."

"Unreasonable," Adrian echoed thoughtfully. "He likes the place that much?"

Ponsonby shook his head as if he was truly bewildered. "That's what I find the most astonishing about it! The tenant doesn't even *like* it where he is. He's miserable, if the truth be told. I'd wager his *family* isn't happy there either. Funny how some people cling to the very thing that is the source of their troubles. Now, what can we do that will help him — and help us?"

Adrian tensed as the game they were playing became clearer. He stared at the scattered maps on the desktop as his mind raced. It was his move in this verbal chess game and he had to make it carefully. "To help *him*, you'd have to give him a way out that will leave him with a sense of dignity. If he gives up the building, he'll have to do it with nothing to be ashamed of. He must have somewhere to go, a *better* position elsewhere, if you catch my meaning."

"An excellent point." Ponsonby nodded.

Adrian added for emphasis, "It's *very* important that he be taken care of properly. Are we agreed on that?"

"That can be arranged. But I've already told you that he doesn't want to go. He won't be persuaded. He's unreasonable. How do we get him out and still leave him with a sense of dignity?" Ponsonby demanded.

Adrian turned away and walked to one of the large windows looking out at the patio. Once again the move was his. Perhaps it was the most important move of all.

Ponsonby stood at Adrian's shoulder. "You've grown a lot

since you came to work for me. I can see it already. You're not some spotty-faced loser. You have potential. You're worth all the time and energy I've put into you. Talk to me, Adrian. How do we do it?"

Adrian's cheeks flushed. They were talking about Christ Church, there was no doubt about it. And Ponsonby had hit the right chord when he had mentioned how miserable his father and the entire family were. It reverberated through all the questions Adrian himself had. Why was his father so determined to hold on to the church? What purpose did it serve except to keep him under the thumbs of the archdeacon and the bishop? *What was the point?* Wouldn't escape be better? Wouldn't it help everyone concerned if Ponsonby could win and build his blasted superstore? *What was the point?* Perhaps if they were all forced to go somewhere else, they could salvage what was left of their relationships. "We need to discover an angle, a bit of information, *something* that will legally take the decision out of the tenant's hands completely," he said.

"For example?"

He didn't want to give too much away. "You say it's an old building. What kind of old building?"

"Why? What does that matter?"

"Because an old building may have structural problems that could contain safety hazards."

Ponsonby smiled again. "You're on the right track, son."

The *son* gave him a momentary pause, but he went on. "If you could have the building inspected and show that it's a health hazard, it would be closed down. If it's a terribly old building and if the tenant isn't wealthy, renovations will be too expensive for him to hope to accomplish."

"Of course," Ponsonby exclaimed. "It makes perfect sense."

Clydesdale spoke for the first time, cleaning his gold-wire spectacles as he did. "A battle over the building is the best way to go," he said in a thick, cultured voice. "We have a chance with that one."

Ponsonby clapped Adrian on the back. "Well done, son, well done. The only thing left is for you to tell us what, precisely, is wrong with your father's church so we may call inspectors in to investigate."

He couldn't look at Ponsonby, and instead fixed his eyes on a spot of green on one of the maps. "Well, *hypothetically speaking*, the church is very old. So a church that old might have problems with its foundation. Maybe it's so old that it's cracking and slipping. It might even be sinking. But I'm not an inspector. I'm just a kid. What do I know?"

Ponsonby sighed. "Hypothetically speaking."

"Right."

"Mr. Clydesdale, will you be able to persuade our local council to grant permission for an inspection? As soon as possible? Tomorrow morning?"

"It won't be a problem," Clydesdale said.

Deep inside, Adrian felt the sense of release that a move had been made that could not be reversed. Everything was set into motion. He clung to the notion that this would lead to nothing but good. His father would be freed from a dead-end job in a dead-end church. It was the best thing for everyone.

"Excellent. Thank you, Clydesdale," Ponsonby said. "And thank *you*, Adrian. You've maintained my faith in you. And for that, I want you to go to York with Lewis to represent me on a bit of business there."

"Represent you?"

"Yes. I have a store that's doing poorly, and I want you to go in and assess the situation for me. Find out what's wrong. Make sure the managers are doing their jobs. Give me your *impressions* about how to salvage the store, improve its profit margin. You're a sharp lad. I trust you."

"Thank you, Mr. Ponsonby."

Ponsonby nodded. "You're welcome. Pack an overnight bag. Lewis will take you immediately."

"Immediately?"

"Yes, if you leave now, you'll be there this afternoon. I'll expect you back sometime tomorrow evening."

With the purposeful stride of someone on a great mission, Adrian headed for the door. He stopped and turned. "I'll need to phone my parents."

"I'll take care of that," Ponsonby said. "You go."

Adrian went. He felt elated and free in that reckless way a child feels when he has thrown himself from a great height into the arms of someone dependable. Mr. Ponsonby would catch him. Mr. Ponsonby would take care of everything.

20

I II III IV V VI VII VIII IX X XI XII

The express bus roared away from the airport, lumbering from one congested road to another until it joined the morning traffic on a multilaned motorway. Once they were pointed west for Bristol, the England Jeff expected to see unfolded before him. Clusters of sun-washed villages nestled on rolling green hills and rich farmland appeared and disappeared beyond the scratched windows of the bus. The tourist map in his lap gave some of them names like Wootton Bassett, Tormarton, Chiseldon, and Pucklechurch. They sailed past larger towns too, like Slough, Reading, and Swindon. But it was hard for Jeff to appreciate his journey. He was frustrated that his cell phone didn't work in a foreign country. And his mind kept going back to Malcolm.

Arthur, meanwhile, had the look of a man who'd returned home after a long trip only to find that someone had built a factory on his old playground.

They reached the city of Bristol in a little over two hours. The bus entered along a main highway that led into a labyrinth of streets toward the city center, crowded with buildings old and new; fancifully florid Victorian churches sat side by side with unimaginative concrete blocks built after World War Two. The clouds had turned so gray that Jeff couldn't tell where the buildings ended and the sky began.

"Bristol is the largest city in southwest England," a prere-corded voice crackled through a distorted sound system. "During the Middle Ages, it was a textile center. You Americans might be interested to know that it was John Cabot's point of departure in 1497 for the New World."

Jeff made a mental note to ask Malcolm who John Cabot was.

The driver continued, "The city thrived on its business with America. Now, situated on the Avon River, about seven miles from the Bristol Channel, it is a major seaport and an international finance center, second only to London. Bristol is known for exporting nuclear machinery, aircraft parts, tobacco, and food products."

On a large oblong stretch labeled St. Augustine's Parade the bus hugged a curb and stopped in front of a concert hall called the Hippodrome. The large marquee advertised a show Jeff had never heard of. The bus driver opened the doors and the passengers filed out.

Arthur stood up, but Jeff nervously blocked his way to the aisle. "We have to stay together," Jeff gestured in as forceful a manner as he could to a man Arthur's size.

Arthur simply smiled at him. They stepped off the bus.

"I have to find a pay phone," Jeff said and scanned the area. He spotted a large red phonebox and turned to tell Arthur to come with him. But Arthur wasn't there. Jeff pivoted and quickly spied his fugitive moving through the crowd down the street.

"Oh no," Jeff groaned and chased after him.

There are times when life is like a movie, Jeff thought as he hustled through the crowd. In a strange city in a foreign country, he suddenly felt like an actor — no, a secret agent — shadowing his nemesis. The heads of the people bobbed up and down like little plastic balls in a bathtub. Jeff ducked and dodged to keep Arthur in view. An easy task considering Arthur's size, but it was made difficult by the pedestrians and traffic crossing Denmark Street.

"Arthur!" Jeff wanted to cry out. But he knew it would be useless.

What's he doing? Jeff wondered with exasperation. *Where does he think he's going? Doesn't he know that he's lost?* Arthur turned a corner and Jeff followed, noting that they were headed up Park Street.

Jeff suddenly slammed into Arthur, who had stopped. He was looking at two homeless derelicts curled up in the fetal position on a bed of rags and whiskey bottles. Arthur knelt next to one and poked gently at the threadbare coat. A tangled mass of hair and leather-like skin lifted up to look at Arthur through tiny, slit eyes.

Arthur said something softly to him.

The derelict swore at Arthur, then lowered his head and went back to sleep.

Arthur slowly stood. Then he gestured with both hands toward the derelicts and then the city. It was a plea that Jeff took to mean, "What has happened here? How can you have people sleeping on the street with all these buildings around?"

Jeff didn't have an answer for him. He grabbed Arthur's arm. "We have to go call Malcolm," he said, balling up his fist and putting it next to his head as if it was a telephone receiver.

Arthur looked at him quizzically, then spun around and walked on up the street. Jeff gritted his teeth and followed along. *How do you reason with a man who won't listen?* he asked himself. *How do you communicate with someone who won't be spoken to?*

Arthur slowed his pace as if he realized he didn't have to worry about escaping from Jeff. He strolled casually up the steep incline. He scrutinized the shops with their window displays of the latest fashions and electronic equipment, and restaurants with large photos of the food they served. Jeff kept an eye out for a phone, but lost hope of finding a way to restrain Arthur long enough to use one.

As they walked, Jeff also noticed that Arthur seemed to look intently into the faces of the people he passed. Some of them responded to his direct eye contact with uncomfortable expressions and annoyance. Once or twice, they recoiled so severely that they almost stumbled from the sidewalk into the street.

"Don't do that!" Jeff whispered harshly.

Arthur cocked a furry eyebrow at him and grinned.

Jeff suddenly had a nagging sense that, for the first time since Arthur arrived in their time, he wasn't simply reacting to his circumstances or stumbling into a haphazard event. Arthur knew what he was doing. There was a *purpose* to this little escapade.

Because Jeff watched Arthur so closely, he didn't notice that the traffic on Park Street dissipated. It was as if someone had turned the tap off and the last few drops — a couple of cars and vans — slid by.

At the top of the street, Arthur stopped to gaze curiously at the Wills Building, a large Gothic building with a square tower and bells. Winded now, Jeff tugged at Arthur's sleeve and tried to make the gestures and sounds he hoped would communicate that they needed to stop for a minute.

Arthur seemed to understand — and maybe they both would have sat down — but Jeff noticed several policemen standing next to their white-and-blue cars ahead of them near a museum and art gallery. Barriers were put up at the intersection, and some of the police were wearing riot gear. Jeff was worried, and was thinking of ways to get away, when a dam broke and a river of people washed out from the top of the street, through the buildings and alleyways toward them. Jeff looked around wildly. There were hundreds of them, some carrying placards and signs. As they drew closer, Jeff realized that the crowd was made up mostly of young faces. Students on the march, Jeff thought with alarm.

Arthur stood with his hands on his hips, like a man daring the tide to come in. The protestors, with shouts and chants, marched at them obliviously. Jeff pushed at him to move to one side but he wasn't interested in getting out of the way. The marchers surrounded them and with the sheer force of their numbers carried Arthur and Jeff back down Park Street.

The signs and placards complained about student's rights being robbed and animal rights being abused and women's rights being thwarted, and Jeff knew that this wasn't a protest against a single problem, but every problem the students could think of. Jeff finally shouted at a young bearded and spectacled man next to him. "What's going on?" Jeff asked. "Why is everybody protesting?"

"The prince," the young man answered. "He's making a speech at the Council House."

"Prince?"

"We want him to know we don't like the way our royalty lives off the backs of the oppressed," he said, then shouted for good measure, "Down with the monarchy!"

Several others picked up the chant, repeating it again and again.

Jeff glanced at King Arthur, glad he didn't understand what kind of protest he'd joined.

"We have to go," Jeff shouted at Arthur, who was looking around at the students with deep interest as they marched.

Again, Arthur gave no sign that he understood or that he was inclined to go anywhere other than where he was at the moment.

Back at the bottom of Park Street, the multitude broke out onto College Green, an expanse of lawn leading to the Council House grounds. The "House" itself was a massive block-long, crescent-shaped building with a moat and majestic fountains.

On one side, a portable stage had been set up for the prince's speech. The police and security personnel watched the approaching throng apprehensively as they gathered around the podium with those who'd already arrived for the event. Everyone pressed in close. Jeff broke out in a sweat, trying to keep an eye on Arthur. Words were loudly exchanged between those who supported the prince and those who didn't. More chanting and sign waving ensued. Jeff had a tight-throated feeling that anything could happen in this electric atmosphere.

Suddenly, a roar went up from the crowd as a group of men in suits mounted the makeshift stand. They were an uneasy procession. A lean, gray-headed, distinguished-looking gentleman approached the microphone and tried to speak above the shouts and jeers. He might've been a dean or a chancellor. Whoever it was, Jeff had a vague sense that he was trying to establish some sense of propriety before introducing the prince. It didn't seem to work. He returned to the rest of the men — one of whom must've been the prince himself, Jeff didn't know for certain — and they consulted about what to do. They appeared to disagree, based on the pointed fingers and shaking heads. Finally, a tall, brown-haired man stepped out from the consultation and moved to the microphone. It was the prince. The crowd screamed both blessings and curses accordingly.

Much later Jeff would think about stories throughout history where the catalyst for a major event turned out to be a single word or a little nudge or an unkind expression. Who fired the first shot at Lexington? What triggered the riot on the Bastille that led to the French Revolution? Who gave the fatal signal at Fort Sumter? And, finally, who started the riot on that gray day in Bristol?

Jeff would never know. What he *did* know was that the student protestors suddenly became a mob and everyone went collectively insane. Factions turned on each other with flying fists and thrown debris. The signs became weapons. People pushed, shoved, and trampled their way across the Green and toward the podium. The prince and his entourage quickly exited and disappeared into the council building. Police whistles blew and sirens wailed.

Jeff grabbed at Arthur's arm and this time he complied. With all the gentleness of a battering ram, Arthur pushed his way across the lawn toward an area that seemed the most deserted. It led to a small street where they jogged left and went around to the rear of the building, away from the noise and the violence. Jeff wondered if ducking into a back door might be the best way to go and gestured toward one. Arthur nodded and they went — past a row of official-looking black cars, reaching the door just as it flew open.

What happened next took no more than a few seconds, but to Jeff it felt like everything shifted into slow motion and a few seconds became minutes.

Two security men stepped through the door and, seeing only Jeff and Arthur, pushed them aside. Jeff, of course, was no problem and fell back easily. Arthur stepped back, watching. The security men were headed to the black cars — and nothing would stop them. The prince emerged through the door and walked confidently, but quickly, past Arthur and Jeff.

Jeff wasn't sure if Arthur had done something to get the prince's attention, but the prince suddenly turned back toward Arthur and they made eye contact. Arthur didn't move, or speak, but the prince's expression suddenly changed. It was as if he had somehow recognized Arthur.

Arthur's expression, on the other hand, was transformed into one of sadness and sympathy. At that point, Arthur *did* say something to the prince in Latin.

The prince tilted his head curiously, pleasantly surprised. There was something about his look that conveyed appreciation to Arthur.

The security agents misjudged the exchange between the

two men and interpreted it as a threat to the prince's person. One threw a hard blow at Arthur's stomach, which only annoyed Arthur, while the other grabbed the prince and dragged him to one of the cars. Arthur grabbed the security man and lifted him up off the ground by his lapels. What Arthur intended to do with him, Jeff didn't know, since a *third* security man — a policeman — gave him a good thump on the back of the head with a baton.

On the ground with Jeff at his side, Arthur rubbed his head as the engines revved and the cars squealed away down the street.

Remnants of the crowd appeared around both sides of the building, and rocks and bottles were thrown angrily at the retreating vehicles. Jeff and Arthur got to their feet. Jeff spun around to look for a way to escape. As he turned, a bottle launched by a student with exceptionally poor aim flew missile-like toward him. He caught sight of it out of the corner of his eye and ducked — but too late. It made a solid connection with the side of his head. A burst of light shattered into tiny pinwheels that spun into oblivion like Fourth of July fireworks.

Everything went black.

21

Sirens wailed somewhere outside, but they didn't compare to the scream inside Jeff's head. He opened his eyes cautiously. He was in an office, stretched out on a lime green sofa he found so offensive he closed his eyes again. He gently eased himself up with a groan and lightly touched the bump where the bottle had hit.

"Easy now," a woman said. She was in a chair next to the sofa and she peered over her reading glasses at him, her elderly white face was crowned with a bush of silver hair. Jeff's immediate impression was that she looked like a librarian.

"Ow. Where am I?" Jeff asked.

"The Old Library."

Jeff swung his legs off the sofa. A dull pain shot through his head.

"Now, not so fast. That's quite a lump you have there," the woman said. "Caught in the riot, were you? A terrible mess. I rang for an ambulance, oh, must've been twenty minutes ago, but they haven't arrived. Probably won't. Worse cases than your bump to deal with, I suppose. Still, I think the police have it under control now."

"Where is he?"

"The man who brought you in?" she asked. "He left."

"What?" Jeff exclaimed, to his regret. A sharp pain shot through his skull. "Owwwww!"

"Now just lie still," she advised.

Jeff spoke more softly. "He's gone."

"Yes," she said sharply. Her tone and expression made Jeff think that she wanted to say more than that. He waited a moment, and she continued with diplomatic effort, "He has a lot to learn about manners, that's certain."

"Where am I?" Jeff asked.

"The Old Library, as I said. Directly across from the Council House. He carried you in and demanded that I help you. Of course, I was only too happy to be of service and find ice for your lump until medical help could arrive. But *your friend* then started lecturing me about the condition of our country: people sleeping in the streets, riots by our young people, monarchs who are stripped of their power and helpless to — "

Jeff held up a hand. "Wait a minute. I'm sorry. He *said* all of that? In *English*?"

"No, not in English. In Latin," she replied.

"You *know* Latin?"

"I should say so. I went to Cambridge! Of course, I thought it was a bit peculiar that he insisted on speaking in Latin. I assumed he was a professor playing a game with me, but he persisted and — "

"But what happened to him? Please. You have to tell me everything he said."

She sighed impatiently. "I *was* telling you. He ranted and raved like a mad man. He blamed *me* personally for the trouble in this country. He said it was quite obvious to him that it was the teachings of the universities that have led to the decay he's seen since arriving. Of all the nerve."

Jeff's head throbbed harder, in time with his confusion. "The teachings of the universities? How does he know about what you teach?"

"By asking, of course," she said, as if that answered everything. "As I said, when he first came in, carrying you and speaking proficient Latin, I assumed he was one of our professors. While I put an icepack on your head, we chatted about the university. It was all quite cordial. He seemed fascinated by the scope of learning here."

Jeff thought back to Arthur on the street, looking at the shops and buildings, studying the faces of the people. *The walk wasn't some kind of impulsive event. There was method to his madness,* Jeff realized. *He was on a fact-finding tour to figure out what had become of his England.* Jeff considered Arthur with a new appreciation. Until that moment, he'd thought of Arthur as a big, uncontrollable, uncivilized brute who'd probably become king by sheer strength and not through any inherent intelligence. But *now* . . .

"He was perfectly cordial until we began to discuss religion," the librarian said.

"Religion?"

"He asked to see the bishop," she said. "It was obvious that he assumed a bishop or other cleric ran the university. I informed him that the church has nothing to do with our university. He was quite shocked. I went even further to say that we no longer require our instructors to believe in God or Jesus Christ. Then he simply lost control. He said that such faithlessness is always at the heart of a nation's downfall — and it often begins with apostate teachers. Honestly, I feared he might resort to physical violence. He said he'd banish us all if he could."

Jeff pressed his hands over his face to hide his smile.

"Is he some sort of fundamentalist?" she asked.

"In a way," Jeff replied.

"He said over and over that it was the fulfillment of prophecy. The bishop was right. The country has been left to godless pagans. To what bishop was he referring?"

"I don't know."

"It was the most remarkable thing," she said, shaking her head so that her loose jowls dangled. "Where did he learn his Latin? It was authentically ancient."

"Didn't he mention who he was?"

"I asked, but he ignored the question. That's when he left. He asked me to take care of you and simply walked out. Not even a word of thanks," she said indignantly.

"Well, thank you from me," Jeff said. Another flick of pain reminded him of his wound. "But he didn't say anything about where he was going?"

"Not a peep," she answered, then said, "You're an American, I assume."

"Yes, ma'am," Jeff answered, and wondered what made her ask at this particular moment.

"This is your first visit to England?"

"Yeah," he said. "We flew in this morning."

"Quite an introduction — arriving for a riot like that."

Jeff nodded agreeably. "It's definitely not in the tour books."

"Well ..." She suddenly stood up. "You seem to be quite recovered. If there's anything further I can do, don't hesitate to ask. Otherwise, I must return to my duties. I believe the police have the crowds under control, if you wish to leave."

On rubbery legs, Jeff also stood. "There's one thing ... if you wouldn't mind ..."

"Yes?" she asked with a cautionary tone.

"May I use your phone? There's somebody I have to call right away."

✿ ✿ ✿

Finding Malcolm was no easy task. Jeff couldn't remember the name of the hotel near the airport and couldn't think what Malcolm might've done after he had realized that Jeff and Arthur were gone. Would he go to the hotel and wait, or try to find them? Even using the telephone was a chore. The phone numbers for information and the operator weren't the same as in America. Finally, after cross-referencing a telephone book for the umpteenth time, Jeff settled on the most obvious course of action: call Mrs. Packer.

Across the transatlantic lines, Jeff could tell she was audibly relieved to hear from him. "Your cousin is beside himself with worry. He called and said he couldn't imagine how to find you. And then he heard about the riots there."

"He knew we went to Bristol?"

"Someone saw you both get on the bus," she said.

"Where's Malcolm now?" Jeff asked.

"At a hotel in Bristol. Probably not far from where you are now."

Thank God, Jeff thought.

"He had hoped you'd have the presence of mind to call me," Mrs. Packer said, sounding pleased to be helpful in this crisis.

Jeff tried to keep the conversation on track. "What hotel?"

"The Royal," she replied.

"Thanks, Mrs. Packer," Jeff said and hung up.

The librarian knew where the Royal Hotel was and gave Jeff detailed directions. Ten minutes later, Jeff stepped into the thick, red velvety and gold-lined reception area. A crystal chandelier twinkled high above him. A desk manager with a thin mustache eyed him suspiciously. Four minutes and three floors after that, Jeff was being embraced by his Malcolm in his hotel room.

"What a nightmare! The two of you disappeared, the riots ..." Malcolm said. After letting go of Jeff, he looked anxiously at the doorway and hallway beyond. "Where is Arthur?"

Jeff grimaced. "The nightmare isn't over. Arthur left and I don't know where he went."

Malcolm's face fell. "Oh no."

"But," Jeff went on, "strangely enough, I think *he* knew where he was going."

Malcolm looked at Jeff inquisitively. "What do you mean?"

"I mean ... I think I should tell you everything that happened after we got off the bus."

22

I II III IV V VI VII VIII IX X XI XII

On a thick bed of grass in the middle of a field, King Arthur folded his arms behind his head and looked up at the moon. It mutely stared back at him with its unblinking eye. Arthur didn't mind. He and the moon had been friends for a long time. And on this cool, clear night when Arthur was too exhausted from walking to go to sleep, he looked to his old friend to comfort him. What else did he have? The day had been a long one. Not because he had walked so many miles — he was a soldier and used to that — but because of this mind-numbingly horrific vision of the future he had seen. Arthur was not a superstitious man, yet he was frightened in an indescribable way. He was scared by the endless gray stone structures that housed the thousands and thousands of people, crammed and congested, their faces reflecting an inner emptiness. Merlin had taught him well to understand the hearts of men, their hunger and need, for it helped him to be a wise and benevolent king. In the great city he had left a few hours before, the hearts he saw were cold and empty. If they contained anything at all it was a silent scream of buried pain, of yearning that could never be satisfied by outward means, and of hope choked by despair. The mob riot and the lost and confused expression of the prince confirmed it. For all of their monumental structures, self-propelling carts, and mechanical birds, they were spirits in bondage.

"For what do they gain if they possess the entire world but lose their own souls?" our Savior had once asked.

Arthur knew the answer. For he himself had possessed Camelot, that world of all worlds, and lost it to those of unfaithful hearts and wicked desires. The Grail was taken away from him and would not be regained. Not in his time. He knew that. If he ever went back, it would be to face Mordred, that dark and monstrous reflection of himself — his own nephew by witchery. This world seemed to be inhabited by hundreds of Mordreds.

"Oh, God!" he cried out at the moon as it stared him down like his own regret. "Why have you brought me here unless it is to restore the Grail, to bring faith to these people, to drive out the faithless, to give them their own glimpse of Camelot? To what end would you show me these things, make me part of this terrible dream, if not to glorify you?"

No words came to him — from God or anyone else.

Still, he would carry on. He knew that much. If indeed there was a purpose to this living dream, he would find it further along in his journey. He wasn't sure how or why, but he knew he would persevere. As a true knight, he had no choice. It was the brave and chivalrous thing to do. It was the Christian thing to do.

Arthur stared at the moon until its light was all he could see. It shone on him then as it had in another golden age when he had valiant knights at a round table, a beautiful queen, and an invincible kingdom. All because a boy had received a sword from a woman. Would the same happen again if the nation saw a similar miracle?

In wonder he drifted to sleep, the once and future king.

23

I II III IV V VI VII VIII IX X XI XII

Myrddin slid his old mystical bones into the second pew at Christ Church in Wellsbridge. It was early in the morning and the church was empty. That suited Myrddin just fine. He enjoyed the unique silence of the ancient church when no one else was around. For him, it seemed to hum with the timeless prayers of God's people. A rosy-cheeked maiden from 1590, a harried soldier from 1817, a struggling smudged-faced miner from 1934 — their whispered entreaties floated and mingled, drenching the cracked walls and bathing the stone altar in grace. Myrddin knelt, gave the sign of the cross, and pressed his face against two gnarled, folded hands.

He prayed, "Glory be to the Father, and to the Son: and to the Holy Ghost ..."

The sudden thud of the door on the far end of the church startled him. He was determined not to be distracted from his prayers and continued.

"As it was in the beginning, is now and ever shall be: world without end. Amen. Praise ye the Lord ..."

Footsteps clicked against the stone floor and echoed throughout the church. Not one set, but several. Low voices mumbled back and forth. Someone was giving instructions and the footsteps scattered in several directions around him. Myrddin frowned but continued to pray.

"O come, let us sing unto the Lord: let us heartily rejoice in the strength of our salvation . . ."

A familiar set of footsteps approached him and an equally familiar hand rested on Myrddin's shoulder. He turned to look into the stricken face of Graham Ridley.

"Myrddin," Graham whispered in a choked voice.

Myrddin knew before Graham said another word.

"The inspectors are here," said Graham. "They're closing down the church."

Myrddin thrust his chin out. "Not until I've finished my prayers."

Graham protested, "But, Myrddin — "

"If you're the man I think you are, you'll kneel here with me and say *your* prayers too," he said. "They wouldn't dare interfere with morning prayers."

"They might," Graham said as he scooted in next to Myrddin.

"They might *try*," the old sage grunted.

To the annoyance of the three inspectors, Myrddin and Graham prayed for an hour. But they prayed without interruption.

✿ ✿ ✿

Jeff had lost count of the number of times they'd gone over the story. All morning, they considered again and again every detail of what had happened since Arthur's arrival in the present time, telling each other what they knew. Malcolm was certain that they'd discover not only where Arthur was headed, but why he was headed there. Jeff was too jet-lagged to think about it.

"We're missing something," Malcolm said as he peeked out of the bathroom. Half of his face was covered with shaving cream. "There's a link we haven't established. None of this has happened by chance."

Jeff pulled the blanket over his head. They'd been up late and, for him, it still felt early, even though the clock announced in bright red numbers that it was nine o'clock. His head still hurt. He was in a bad mood. "I don't care," he announced.

"From the very beginning, there's been *something*, something, something ..." Malcolm mused on the word *something* several times as he disappeared back into the bathroom.

Under the covers, Jeff's mind clicked into gear against his will. He opened his eyes and looked deep into the cave-like darkness the folds of the bedcovers created. *Something was missing, a link.* The phrase echoed around in his brain, like a lone voice in that cave he imagined. Jeff resisted the urge to explore the idea any further. He wanted to go back to sleep. But the phrase continued to bounce around and the image of a cave transformed to a dark ruin. Like the ruin Malcolm had set up in his historical village. He remembered what had happened the last time he was there. He and Elizabeth had taken the sword and clothes to hide in the stone table. Both had disappeared.

Jeff threw the covers away from his head. So much had happened since then that he hadn't thought about it. *Did they slip back through a crack in time?* he wondered, then asked out loud.

Malcolm stuck his head out from the bathroom. "What?"

"The sword and the clothes. Why did they disappear like that? Was it some kind of magic?"

"Magic has nothing to do with this."

"Then what happened? Did they go back to Arthur's time?"

"Perhaps they did. If the church ruin is where the time fault somehow opened, then maybe it opened again to allow the sword and clothes to slip back through."

"Why?"

"I can't say exactly. Why is *any* of this happening? I don't know."

"But the church ruin is at the center of all this, right? It's where Arthur woke up when he first got here. It's where he ran when he escaped from the hospital. It's where he told Alan to have us hide his stuff."

"What are you thinking, Jeff?"

He replied with another question. "Where did the church ruin come from?"

"Here in England, of course, but — " Malcolm stopped and came out of the bathroom completely. He wore a T-shirt and jeans. "Wait a minute. I believe you're onto something."

"I know it's crazy, but what if Arthur wasn't supposed to show up in Fawlt Line? What if the only reason he showed up there was because — "

"I moved the church ruin from here in England." Malcolm slapped an open palm against his forehead. "Good heavens, where has my brain been?"

Jeff sat up. "Where did the church ruin come from?"

"The ruin came from a tiny village called Wellsbridge." Malcolm gestured toward the small writing desk in the corner of the room. "There's a road atlas. Take a look while I finish shaving. If I remember correctly, it's not far from here."

A moment later, Jeff had checked through the index and opened to the proper page number. "It looks like Wellsbridge is south, maybe southwest from here. Not very far," he called out.

Malcolm joined Jeff at the desk. "Where?"

"Right there." Jeff's finger followed a red line — an "A" road — from Bristol down to the tiny print that said *Wellsbridge*.

"Interesting," Malcolm said and tugged at his ear.

Jeff pondered the map. "It doesn't look very big. It's near — what's this town? — Glastonbury."

"Glastonbury!" Malcolm exclaimed.

"What's the matter?"

"Glastonbury is where Arthur was supposedly buried — or, if you believe the other legend, the Lady of the Lake transported his body in a mysterious ship to some kind of paradise."

"Yeah, but those are just legends," Jeff said.

"Legends often have a basis in fact."

Jeff drew an invisible circle on the map with his finger. "It's all in the same area."

"Then we now know where we have to go."

Jeff and Malcolm got dressed, packed up, checked out of the hotel, and climbed into the white Vauxhall in the parking garage. Jeff felt odd getting in on the left-hand side and *not* face a steering wheel.

The sun drenched the city in a clear light that gave sharp definition to the buildings and blue sky. *No riots today*, Jeff thought as they passed Park Street and the university buildings. Apart from a few boarded windows, there was nothing to indicate that anything had happened the day before.

Malcolm eased the car through Bristol's midday traffic. After a long silence, he said, "Do you see that green car behind us?"

Jeff glanced back. "What about it?"

"It's been following us since we left the hotel."

❁ ❁ ❁

"Sit down, sit down," the archdeacon said and gestured to Graham from beyond his enormous oak desk.

Graham declined the offer. He shifted from one foot to another in agitation. This was the moment he'd been dreading since he became vicar of Christ Church: demanding funds to rebuild his church. "Neville, we have to talk."

"We certainly do," The archdeacon said. "Imagine the embarrassing position in which I was placed to learn from a *layman* that your church has a crumbling foundation. Why didn't *you* tell me?"

Graham was thrown by this sudden reversal. He stammered, "With respect, Neville, I did — or tried to. I've reported that the church is in terrible condition."

"Forgive me," the archdeacon said without sounding contrite. "The phrase *terrible condition* is a far cry from the extreme condition of your church. The foundation is *sinking*, Graham. How could you let it happen?"

"I didn't *let* it happen, Neville." How did this become *his* fault, he wondered. How did the archdeacon — and Ponsonby — find out about the church's foundation?

"I suppose you're here to ask the bishop for money."

Graham leaned on the back of the ornate guest chair for support. "Well, yes, I am. If we don't get repairs underway immediately, Ponsonby will use this as an excuse to build his superstore."

"You have no one to blame but yourself if that happens," the archdeacon said sharply. "The bishop isn't pleased."

"If he isn't pleased, then he must appreciate the seriousness of the situation," Graham said.

The archdeacon fixed his gaze on Graham. "He appreciates it and is at a loss as to what should be done about it."

"Repairing the church is the obvious choice."

"Obvious to you, perhaps, but not to those who must manage the very limited funds of the church. With so many pressing needs, we simply can't see our way clear to invest a lot of money in a church with such a small congregation. Case closed, I'm afraid."

Graham was prepared for an argument, but not such a direct shutdown. It immediately brought him to one conclusion. "Ponsonby got to you, didn't he?"

"I beg your pardon?"

"Has he already made you an offer?"

The archdeacon frowned. "Be very careful what you imply, Graham. Your situation isn't secure."

"Of course it isn't. It never has been." Sweat beaded on Graham's forehead as the simple truth dawned on him. "Moving me from Bristol to Wellsbridge was always part of the plan, wasn't it? Move me to Christ Church, and when the time came you could get rid of us both. You've always known about the sinking foundation, haven't you?"

The archdeacon rolled his eyes. "Don't be paranoid. You make it sound like a conspiracy. Next you'll be saying we shot JFK."

"This whole thing seems terribly convenient," Graham said in a dry, raspy voice.

"If it's convenient, it's only because you made it so. Your conduct — your *son's* conduct — has contributed greatly to our present decision. If you were on this side of the desk you'd see that. Even if we had the money, which we don't, we'd be fools to pour it into Wellsbridge. It's a *dead* church! Why not sell the land to Ponsonby if he can use it? It'll certainly fund ministry opportunities elsewhere." It was an iron-clad argument and the archdeacon knew it.

"And if I raise the money for the repairs myself?"

The archdeacon smiled. "Then I'll give up everything they taught me in seminary and believe in miracles once again. You can't do it. Not in the amount of time we have."

"Amount of time?"

"Three days. The bishop is leaving for Africa and wants the matter settled before he goes. If you want to save your little church, you have three days, Graham."

⚙ ⚙ ⚙

Graham walked into an empty kitchen. Christ Church was framed in the window above the sink. He felt guilty, as if he owed the old building an explanation. He wanted to say that he'd been a pawn and didn't even realize it until it was too late. He wanted to confess that he had failed. He wanted to ask the church for absolution.

"Anne? Adrian?" he called out to the muffled silence. No answer. He was relieved. He wasn't up for explaining to his wife and son how badly he'd botched it — how the church would be torn down and he would be out of a job. Anne would be upset, but strong. Adrian would probably grin and say he knew all along it would end this way. Graham was played for a fool.

Little wonder, then, that Adrian rebelled. Little wonder that Adrian didn't respect him at all. He thought back to their conversations on the way home from the train station and when they worked together on the church. It was as if Adrian knew even then what was happening. Adrian saw what Graham refused to see.

Graham leaned forward on the table. His eye caught the open newspaper spread out in front of him. Anne had written a note with an arrow pointing to one of the articles in the lower right-hand corner of the page. "Thought you'd be interested," Anne's note said.

Graham looked at the article. "Arthur Arrives in England," the headline shouted boldly. Underneath, a short article went on to say that a man calling himself Arthur Pendragon arrived from America the previous morning at Heathrow Airport. Investigation by the reporter revealed that he was the same Arthur who'd been knocked off of a horse several days before in America and had been arrested as a public nuisance. Details were sketchy about how he'd escaped from the mental ward where he had been detained, but apparently he'd gotten a passport and flew to England with two other persons of unknown identity. He was currently at large somewhere near Bristol. The Home Office said they would inquire into the legitimacy of the report.

Myrddin will be interested, Graham thought.

The back door opened and Anne walked in. "Hello, darling," she said.

Graham grunted.

She carried two grocery bags which she deposited on the counter. She didn't bother to unpack them, turning to Graham instead. "I suppose the meeting with the archdeacon didn't go very well."

"It went very well indeed — if you're the archdeacon," Graham said.

"I'm sorry." She moved next to him and caressed the back of his head and neck. "Have you thought about what you might do?"

"I have to raise the money somehow if I'm going to save the church," he answered. "I suppose I could go door-to-door around Wellsbridge and ask my parishioners to help. That'll yield around eight pounds. Otherwise I don't know what to do."

Anne slid into his lap like she did when they were first married. She wrapped her arms around him. "Oh, Graham ..." she said sympathetically.

Graham couldn't look into her eyes. "I feel so foolish, Anne. Where am I going to come up with the kind of money we need to fix the church? How can I hope to battle Ponsonby on that level?"

Anne nuzzled her head against the curve of his shoulder. She spoke softly, "Maybe you shouldn't try to fight Ponsonby that way. Maybe you shouldn't try to fight the way others fight."

"What do you mean?"

"I've been thinking all morning about it," she said with a sigh, then sat up to face him again. "You're not terribly shrewd when it comes to politics. It's not a game you play very well. They make you nervous and sweaty. Which is precisely why a political machine like the archdeacon has been able to manipulate you so effectively."

Graham waited a moment. "Yes — and?"

"The same goes for money," she continued. "Ponsonby has all the money in the world. He lives it and breathes it. You don't. And to think that you'll be able to take him on that way ... well, he'll hang you out to dry."

"Your confidence in me is overwhelming," Graham said.

"You're a kind-hearted *pastor*, Graham," she said softly and reasonably. "Fight with the thing you *do* know about. Fight this in the *spiritual* realm."

Graham laughed. "Spiritual? I'm sorry, but I don't see that the *spiritual* fits into this at all."

"I don't believe my ears. Aren't you the one who always taught that in every situation, the spiritual aspects are the most important ones to consider?"

Graham merely shook his head. "It's not so easy this time."

Anne slid from his lap and went to the counter to unload the grocery bags. "The church's foundation is slipping. Does that mean *your* foundation is slipping too?"

Graham didn't answer. She had zeroed in on the heart of the problem, but he was helpless to respond.

She unpacked the bags with her back to him. "Darling, you're a man of *faith* — of prayer. There was a time when it used to shine from you like no one I'd ever known. You once believed in miracles. Where is your faith now? *What do you believe, Graham?*"

He took his collar off and tossed it onto the table. "I believe in what I see. The politically and financially powerful are the ones who control everything."

"And miracles?"

"Not likely," he said.

He looked out the window toward the church again. His sense of guilt rushed back at him — not only for his failure to save the building, but for not mustering the faith he knew he should have. What kind of miracle could he hope for now?

Just then Graham saw a tall man with long hair and a beard rounding the corner of the church tower. He seemed to be examining the church.

"I thought the city inspectors left," Graham said.

"They did."

Graham sighed. "Then I wonder who this character is."

24

I II III IV V VI VII VIII IX X XI XII

Graham found the stranger poking around the site where the oldest part of the church had been. He was a large man. *A Viking in a modern suit*, Graham thought as he approached him. Something about him made Graham think he was a tourist. Wellsbridge got those every now and then, mostly when they'd lost their way to the more popular Glastonbury and its ancient abbey.

"Can I help you?" Graham asked.

Startled, the man turned to Graham and stood silently with his hands on his hips. He eyed Graham carefully as if he hoped to recognize him.

"The church is closed for repairs. I'm sorry for any inconvenience," Graham said. Graham noticed that, though the man's clothes were nice, they looked wrinkled and dirty. *Homeless*, he thought. A derelict.

The stranger asked Graham a question.

Graham was surprised. Like so many people of his generation, Graham had to learn Latin as part of his classical education. But it had been a long time since he heard anyone speak the language, and he certainly didn't expect it from this man. He had to translate the question slowly in his mind. It was: *Why is the church locked?*

"I told you — " Graham began in English.

The stranger interrupted him with a disapproving wave. "Speak thou in *my* language," the man said.

Graham thought it was some kind of joke. How could *his* language be Latin? Graham stammered, "All right. I'll have to speak slowly because I don't know Latin very well."

"As you wish."

"The church is closed," Graham explained. "It needs repairs to its foundations."

The stranger frowned. "What, pray tell, has become of this part of the church?"

Graham constructed the sentence in his mind, then carefully spoke, "It was dismantled and sold to someone in America."

The stranger nodded. "I have seen it."

Graham tensed. This was a joke, a trick, or the man was a few degrees short of a right angle. "Who sent you? Why are you here?" Graham demanded.

The stranger reached into his jacket pocket and produced a colorful tourist's map of the area. He unfolded it and pointed to Glastonbury.

"Glastonbury," Graham said. So he was a tourist.

"By what name is this town known?" the man asked.

"This is Wellsbridge," Graham answered, then pointed to where the name should have been on the map, but wasn't. It was too insignificant.

The stranger folded the map up again and shoved it in his pocket. "'Tis a fine church and beautiful. Lock it not. It is the house of the most Holy God and should be open to all."

Graham smiled ironically. "Tell that to the inspectors."

The stranger looked at him curiously. "I shall return," he said and walked away from the church — in the direction of Glastonbury.

Graham watched him go — and only then became aware of a low hum emanating from the pile of stones and debris next to the wall of the church. He listened for a moment, trying to discern what it was, but it soon faded. He returned to his house to strategize how to battle Ponsonby.

"Hi, Mum. It's me," Adrian said above the roar of the motorway traffic.

"Where are you?" Anne asked. Even at that distance, Adrian heard the stiffness in her voice.

"On the M5 near Droitwich, I think," he shouted down the phone. "I'm on my way back from York."

Silence on the line for a moment, then, "You haven't heard, I suppose."

"Heard what?"

"The church was overrun with inspectors this morning. They found out about the foundation. It's been closed."

"Oh," Adrian said, his voice catching in his throat. Ponsonby worked faster than he'd thought possible.

"You're not surprised," his mom said.

Adrian tried to deflect her statement. "How did Dad react?"

"He spoke with the archdeacon about getting money for repairs. The archdeacon said no. It seems that the site for the church will be sold to Ponsonby and your father will be out of work."

Adrian wasn't sure he'd heard right. "Out of work? Surely they'll send him to another church."

Was it the phone line or did his mother's voice go cold? "The archdeacon made it fairly clear that he wouldn't be given another church."

"No! They wouldn't do that him!" Adrian cried out. There must be a mistake. He had an agreement with Ponsonby.

"Sorry, but I believe they *would* do that to him," she said. "No doubt you're pleased."

"Pleased?"

"This justifies the lack of respect you have for your father. Your *boss* has won," she said. Icicles formed on the line. "You made the right choice."

"Mum — " he began.

"Don't 'mum' me, Adrian," she snapped. "Maybe one day I'll understand you. But right now I don't." The line clicked loudly as she hung up.

Adrian leaned with his forehead against the cold metal of the phone box. Something had gone wrong. Ponsonby must've made a mistake. His dad was supposed to lose the church, but not his *job*.

Lewis appeared at Adrian's side. "Well, lad?"

"I have to talk to Ponsonby," he said.

❍ ❍ ❍

"Mr. Ponsonby!" Adrian called out as he entered Ponsonby's study.

Ponsonby was at his desk, clicking away on a computer keyboard. He didn't look up. "Oh, good. You're back. How did it go in York?"

Adrian stood at the head of the desk. "I'm not here to talk about York. I want to talk to you about the church."

Ponsonby pushed himself away from the keyboard. He slumped casually into his chair, his hands folded calmly across his chest. "You've already heard. Too bad. I wanted to tell you the good news myself."

"Good news!"

"Of course," Ponsonby said. "We should have this sewn up in no more than three days."

Adrian struggled against Ponsonby's self-assurance. "But what about my dad?"

"What about him?"

"My mother thinks he's out of a job," Adrian explained. "They won't assign him to another church."

Ponsonby looked genuinely concerned. "Really? That's too bad."

Adrian cleared his throat. He needed to be calm, like Ponsonby. "Mr. Ponsonby, it was my understanding that you would make arrangements with the archdeacon for my father's transfer to another church."

"Where on earth did you get that understanding?" Ponsonby asked, incredulously.

"From our meeting. When I told you about the church."

Ponsonby shook his head. "I'm sorry, Adrian, but you had the *wrong* understanding."

"No, sir," Adrian said firmly. "You were going to take care of my father."

Ponsonby spread his arms. "Who do you think I am, the Archbishop of Canterbury? I can't interfere with the policies of the church."

"Rubbish!"

"I can't tell them how to manage their clerics," he went on.

"*Rubbish* again. It was part of the deal. You got what you needed to close the church providing my father was taken care of. We stood right *here* and you agreed. You lied to me."

Ponsonby sat up sharply as if he might fly out of the chair at Adrian. "I didn't lie, Adrian."

"You have another name for it, then?" Adrian asked caustically.

This time Ponsonby did come out of his chair, but not at Adrian. He turned to the large French windows. "I didn't want to have to tell you, but I will to save my own name. I talked to the archdeacon about your father and he blatantly *refused* to transfer him to another church."

"Why?"

"Your father isn't wanted anymore," Ponsonby stated. "They've been planning his dismissal for a long time."

"I don't believe it."

Ponsonby turned to face Adrian. "You must understand something about your father. He may be capable with people, but he's awful at the things that really count in our society."

"Like what?"

"Maneuvering, back-scratching, and making the right friends."

"You mean politics," Adrian said.

"Why are you acting so surprised? Didn't our time together teach you anything? We talked about people like your father. Weren't you taking notes? They don't survive in our world."

"What happens to them then?"

Ponsonby shrugged. "Frankly, I have no idea. I don't keep company with such people."

"That's cruel."

"Cruel or not, I'm telling you the truth." He returned to his desk and sat down. "Listen, Adrian. You have a choice to make about what you believe in — *who* you believe in — and that choice will guide you into the future. Are you following your father's path — or mine?"

"Your wife is right, you know," Myrddin said to Graham as he poured their tea.

"I thought you'd say that."

Myrddin sat down across from him. "All our battles are spiritual in nature. You know that. This one included."

Graham stirred his tea silently. The spoon rattled against the side of the cup.

Myrddin continued on. "Though I suspect it's not the battle you think it is."

Graham looked across at him. "I'm trying to save the church."

"Are you? Why?" he asked.

"Because it's worth saving," Graham said.

"Why?"

Graham thought about it a moment. "It's a good church, beautiful in its own way. The people of Wellsbridge deserve their own church."

Myrddin leaned forward and rested his elbows on the creaky wood table. "I don't believe you. This isn't about a building."

"Isn't it? Why not?" Graham asked, hoping to get to whatever this conversation was *really* about.

"Because it's an average church in appearance, not historically significant in an obvious way, and most of the church-going people in Wellsbridge would be just as happy in a church at Glastonbury or Wells," Myrddin answered simply.

"You're not terribly encouraging."

"I'm trying to discern your heart, Graham. Why do you want to save this church so badly?"

Graham closed his eyes wearily. Why was he here with the old man? Why wasn't he out trying to raise money? "Because it ... it'll save my job."

"So this is merely an exercise to maintain your vocation?"

"No," Graham said impatiently. "It's more than that. If I save the church, I'll save ... me."

"You."

"Yes."

They looked at each other silently as a clock ticked on the mantelpiece. Graham wasn't sure how far he wanted to go with this conversation. He was very tired. Confess and get it over with, he decided. "I think Anne hit the nail on the head when she said that the church's foundation was crumbling and so was mine. She asked me what I believe, Myrddin, and I couldn't answer her. My foundation is in a sorry state. And somehow it seems that ... if I can restore the church, then maybe I'll feel restored too."

Myrddin smiled. "Now I think we're getting closer to the truth. How do you propose to save the church and yourself? By spending the next three days trying to raise money that no one you know has?"

"If that's what it takes," Graham said.

"But will that save you or will that merely reinforce what you already cynically believe?" Myrddin asked.

"Eh?"

"You've picked up the confused notion that money and power are the only ways to survive in this world."

"Experience can be a great teacher," Graham said sarcastically.

"A great teacher, but a rotten god."

"What?"

Myrddin laughed. "By all means, be taught by experience, but not to the exclusion of the power of God. Things are happening, Graham. We're on the edge of a wondrous time. A time of miracles."

Graham wanted to believe him.

"Did you see the article in the paper?" Myrddin asked.

"Yes."

"Arthur's here."

Graham groaned. "It's a *tabloid* article, Myrddin. Last week they said aliens had kidnapped the prime minister's brain."

"Ah, but this is true."

"How do you know?"

"I can *feel* it. He's here." Myrddin's eyes were wide with awe. Graham thought then as he had often thought: that if he weren't so close to the old man, he'd write him off as mad.

Graham chose his words carefully. "Myrddin, forgive me. You had me going for a minute there. I was beginning to believe that whole bit about wondrous times and miracles. But I can't believe in this nonsense about Arthur. If you're trying to make a connection between my struggling faith and the arrival of a mythological king, don't bother. It won't happen. It *can't* happen."

"And you're the wise sage who is going to tell God what he can or cannot do? *Est autem fides credere quod nondum vides; cuius fidei merces est videre quod credis*!" he shouted.

Faith is to believe what you do not see; the reward of this faith is to see what you believe, Graham translated. The Latin made him think of the stranger at the church. "Why is everyone speaking Latin at me today?"

"You've convinced yourself to believe in money and power, so that's all you see. But you can see so much more if you'll see with your faith. Perhaps if you — " Myrddin suddenly stopped. "Who's been speaking to you in Latin?"

Myrddin's quick interest surprised Graham. "A tourist who

stopped by the church. Homeless, I thought, except that he insisted that we speak in Latin. Awfully peculiar. He was on his way
to Glastonbury."

"Glastonbury," Myrddin mused.

Graham decided to get things back on track so he could
leave. "Look, Myrddin, everything you say *sounds* good but, for
now, they sound like idealistic words. I don't know how to make
them work in this situation."

Myrddin half-smiled as he stood up. "You want to see? Come
walk with me."

Graham declined. "I don't have time. I have to call a meeting
of the church committee."

"The committee will wait. Walk with me."

"Myrddin — "

"If not for the sake of your soul, then come for the sake of our
friendship," Myrddin challenged him.

"You're a strange old man," Graham said with affectionate
annoyance, looking at Myrddin the way he always did when he
was about to give in. "Why should I?"

Myrddin placed a hand on his shoulder. "To see with your
eyes what your absence of faith won't let you see."

27

I II III IV V VI VII VIII IX X XI XII

Arthur, son of Uther and Igraine, apprentice to Merlin, and legendary king of Britain entered Glastonbury with a heavy heart and weary legs just as the clouds gathered for a downpour. Never had he felt more tired and alone. The constant assault of unfamiliar sights and times, a strange language, and uncertain mission bore down on him. Worse were the moments when he thought he *had* recognized an area of land, only to find it marred with black roads, houses, and buildings.

Glastonbury brought the most mixed feelings of all. It had originally been a beautiful settlement village on an island called Avalon. Arthur knew it well. Avalon was the cradle of Christianity in Britain. Joseph of Arimathea, Arthur's direct ancestor and the man who owned the tomb Jesus Christ had been buried in, had traveled there with eleven disciples in the first century to spread the gospel of Christ. He brought with him the chalice used by Jesus at his last supper before his crucifixion and resurrection.

The story was told that one Christmas morning, Joseph wearily sat down and stuck his staff into the ground. It sprouted and blossomed into a hawthorn bush. The miracle of his staff was interpreted by him and his disciples that they were to stop their journeying and build a church dedicated to the chalice. Arthur himself had worshiped at the church, often at Christmas when the bush flowered year after year in memory of the birth of Jesus.

More recently, it was also the site where the evil Melwas had kidnapped Queen Guinevere, Arthur's wife. Arthur laid siege to the castle and, had it not been for the compassionate intercessions of that great man of God, Gildas, the end would have been in spilled blood and painful death. Guinevere was freed without harm. Arthur was pleased to remember that, later, Lancelot had a conflict with Melwas and killed him in single combat. Justice had been served after all.

But now all was different. Avalon the island had been replaced by Glastonbury the town. Arthur struggled to identify what was left. From the point where he first approached the town, he saw Tor Hill. Like everything else, it had changed. Tor Hill now had a stone tower on top. When it had been built or why was more than Arthur could guess.

Arthur walked along a road that took him deeper into congested traffic and crowds of tourists. He felt uncomfortable and out of place stuck in the middle of the strangely dressed crowd, with their unusual headwear, black eye coverings, and small boxes that they continually pressed against their faces. He braved it. For no sensible reason, he had it in mind that somehow he'd learn more of his mission if he went to the center of town, though he didn't know how or from whom. He turned right onto the High Street — which had been blocked off to traffic — and weaved his way past the gift shops, restaurants, banks, and newsagents. He caught sight of a storefront that had been set up as a tourist display. The tapestries and paintings intrigued him because they were so unlike the color posters and photographs he had seen plastered to every available space. These were more in the style of art from Arthur's time. He walked into the building to look around.

Arthur quickly concluded that it was a place to commemorate the town's history. He went to a counter and rifled through the stacks of folded paper there, looking for a map. He succeeded and tried to discern where he was in conjunction with the other things he'd hoped to see. Since the map was in English, he used the positions of the three hills to help him remember. To his delight, he found a mark for the Chalice Well, known better to Arthur as the *Chalk* Well. That would be as good of a starting point as any — if only to see what they'd done to the landmarks he cherished the most.

He turned to leave the building but glimpsed a glass-encased display with Latin writing. He went to it with hopes that it might tell him even more than the nonsensical literature scattered around the room.

The display contained reproductions of old manuscripts. It took him a moment to realize that the display was about the life of King Arthur — *his* life. He laughed at the inaccurate retelling of his battle against invading Romans, particularly when the story claimed that the Romans were giants. He was then surprised to find himself moved by the account of how he had banished Lancelot after finding out that Lancelot and Guinevere were adulterers. He didn't want to read any more.

Yet he couldn't pull himself away. For the first time, it occurred to him that from the vantage point of the future, he could find out how he ultimately died. Was it of old age? Perhaps he died in his sleep after restoring his kingdom to its former glory. His heart trembled anxiously as he followed the sequence of pictures and writings to their conclusion. Most of them were in English, but a final matted picture of an ancient manuscript had enough Latin for Arthur to read.

Legend says that King Arthur and his wicked nephew Mordred fatally wounded one another in battle ... the display had read.

He clenched his fists, crumpling the map as he spun away from the display, out the front door, and onto the pedestrian mall. *Slain by Mordred!* he cried within himself. The words burned through his body like fever in his veins. *Slain by Mordred.* So that was the end of the battle he was going to fight when this nightmare began. ·

Arthur pushed his way back down High Street in the same direction he'd come. At that moment he needed to see and to touch something from his own time. He needed comfort and knew that there was one place in Glastonbury where he'd find it.

Arthur anxiously walked south on Chilkwell Street and unhappily joined a crowd of tourists who had come to see what he'd hoped to see: the Chalk Well. He felt claustrophobic as they entered through a manicured garden and followed a path to a small stone wall with a lion's head carved in the center. Water, from an unknown source, streamed from the lion's mouth.

The well, Arthur thought, relieved. It didn't look the same as it had in his time, but he was grateful that someone hadn't built a large building on it. The water still flowed from some mysterious spring deep beneath the Mendip Hills. Arthur pressed forward to touch the water, to wash his face with it, to drink in its healing powers. He was squeezed out by the other tourists who clamored to get cups and glasses under the spout for a drink. Arthur watched angrily. Their vacant smiles and incessant chatter made his blood boil. Didn't they understand where they were? Didn't they realize how sacred this place was? It was here that blood-colored water poured out to bring healing to the sick and infirmed. Joseph of Arimathea himself brought about the miracle! This entire area was holy ground and should be dealt with respectfully!

His fists still clenched, Arthur raised them to strike out at the disrespectful crowd. He wanted to teach them respect and honor. He wanted to thrust them all aside so he could treat the well with the reverence it was worthy to receive.

At that moment, the threatening clouds above yielded their rain in large, heavy drops that soon opened into a deluge. The tourists scattered for shelter. Arthur thankfully watched them go and used the intervening seconds to calm himself down. *Legend* said he was slain by Mordred. But legend wasn't always right. Perhaps there was another end the legends didn't know about. Perhaps Arthur thwarted Mordred. Perhaps Arthur could *still* thwart Mordred somehow. In his heart, he didn't believe it. The legend was true.

Empty of the tourists, Arthur knelt at the well. The rain poured down his bent head, and his clothes were quickly soaked through and through. Muddied rivulets mixed with tears and ran into his sleeves from his clasped hands. Oblivious, he prayed.

The rain continued to fall as Arthur emerged from the garden and followed Chilkwell Street up to a large park-like area. He crossed the road, dodging the cars as he did, and entered the park. He kept his gaze fixed on the place where the church of Joseph of Arimathea had once stood. It was gone. Now there stood several tall ruins of churches Arthur didn't recognize. He was a man out of place and time, he remembered. How many churches had been built and destroyed? What truly had become of the people Arthur knew and loved the most? They were buried deep in places of fallen stone and thick moss.

Where had *he* been buried if he had been toppled by a thrust of Mordred's sword?

Arthur sat down on the cold, wet stone steps under the arch of one of the ruins. He wished this dream would end. He wished he could return to his own time. Knowing now that his battle with Mordred would be fatal, he could return to alter the events: change the day of the battle, make peace with Mordred, or perhaps have Mordred assassinated in his sleep. But he was helpless to do anything at all until he could go back to his time. *God, why am I here?* he asked as he put his face in his hands. He was a forlorn figure in the gray rain.

A hand fell lightly onto his shoulder. "My friend," a voice said in Latin.

Arthur lifted his head slowly and looked up into the face of Merlin.

28

I II III IV V VI VII VIII IX X XI XII

"It's you, isn't it?" Myrddin asked with misty eyes.

"God save us," Arthur gasped.

Myrddin smiled, barely able to keep from dancing among the ruins. "You *do* speak Latin. Of course you would. What other language would you know? Ancient Celtic perhaps? Latin."

Arthur leapt to his feet and embraced Myrddin in a bone-crunching hug. "I prayed to God for help. He has answered my prayers. Thou art here, old friend."

Graham, who'd been standing several feet away, took a few steps forward. He was afraid the hug might turn into something more violent.

"Is this your tourist from the church?" Myrddin asked Graham after Arthur returned him to his own two feet.

Graham nodded. "What's this all about?"

Myrddin patted Arthur on the arm and spoke slowly in Latin. "Sire, I would like you to meet the Reverend Graham Ridley, the priest of Christ Church in Wellsbridge."

Arthur bowed. "I was lost and this good man gave me aid but this morning. I am grateful to you."

"A pleasure," Graham said quickly, then turned to Myrddin. "Myrddin? What's going on here?"

"Graham," Myrddin began, but stopped. The words caught in his throat as tears of happiness spilled from his eyes. He quickly brushed them aside. "Forgive me. I'm proud to introduce you to … King Arthur."

Graham tilted his head forward and rubbed his eyes wearily. "Oh, God, have mercy on the feeble-minded."

"What?" Myrddin exclaimed. "You still don't believe?"

Graham sucked in his breath as if it was the only way to control his anger. "I'm going back to Wellsbridge. I only hope I can catch a cab," Graham said and walked away.

"What will it take to make you believe!" Myrddin called after him. His voice was deadened by the rainfall around the ruins.

A tall, thin man with an open umbrella stepped out from under an archway. "Perhaps I can help," he said.

Graham spun around to see who spoke.

A boy, probably in his late teens, appeared next to the man with the umbrella. He looked wet and slightly bewildered.

"My name is Malcolm Dubbs," the man said simply. "I believe we all have a lot to talk about."

Arthur raised his face to the rain and laughed.

✿ ✿ ✿

The five of them gathered in a room at an inn Malcolm had found between Glastonbury and Wellsbridge. The rain lashed at the window as they drank hot coffee, tea, and, for Arthur, a large ale. Malcolm explained to an enthusiastic Myrddin and a skeptical Graham everything that had happened and the various theories they'd had along the way about *why* it was happening. Myrddin translated the account to Arthur who, considering his despondency at the abbey ruin, now seemed happy in a childlike way.

"It's obvious that he was displaced in time," Malcolm said in conclusion. "Though we haven't been able to figure out exactly why. We guessed only that he belonged here in England and got him here. The rest is still a mystery."

Graham remembered meeting Malcolm briefly when he'd come to purchase the church ruin. That had seemed indulgent.

This was insane. "You seem like mature, reasonable men — for Americans — and I can't believe what I'm hearing. You honestly believe that this man is Arthur and he's come shooting through time for ... for some sort of mission?"

Malcolm nodded. "Exactly."

"Why?" Graham challenged. "Why is he here?"

"I called him," Myrddin said.

All eyes turned to the old man as he translated in Latin for Arthur.

"I called you," he repeated in Latin and then English. "I blew the horn that called you from the Cave of Dreams."

"The Cave of Dreams?" Malcolm asked. "What is that?"

Myrddin thought for a moment, and then said, "It is where the reality of the past resides in the dreams of the present."

"What's that mean?" Jeff asked.

Myrddin replied, "I suppose, in your terminology, you'd call it a crack in time or a fault line. I never questioned *how* King Arthur would return. I simply knew in faith that he would. God often sends us help in the most peculiar ways."

"And in the most peculiar places. Arthur wound up in *America* rather than here," Malcolm said.

"Part of the mystery," Myrddin said with an impish smile.

Jeff raised his hand as if he were in school. "Wait a minute: help? Who needs his help?" Jeff asked.

Myrddin said, "Britain needs Arthur now more than ever."

"Why now?" Graham had a look on his face that said he was playing along, but not believing any of it.

"You more than anyone should know the answer to that question," Myrddin said to Graham with a hint of rebuke.

Arthur, a sad expression on his face, spoke to Myrddin, who replied — and they went back and forth for a moment, a low, but tense, exchange. Finally, Arthur slammed his hand against the table with a loud exclamation, rattling the cups and saucers.

Graham interrupted. "You have a non-Latin-speaking audience, Myrddin."

Myrddin sighed deeply. "He rebuked me for disappearing and leaving him all alone. He wants to know where I've been."

"He believes you're Merlin?" Jeff asked.

Myrddin nodded. "He believes I'm here to help him in his fight against Mordred. He is convinced of it. I told him that this isn't a battle of strength, but of character and honor. It's a spiritual battle of sorts. I asked him if he is prepared to fight such a battle."

"But what do you mean, a spiritual battle?" Graham asked impatiently. "And don't tell me I should know better than anyone else because I *don't* know."

"That," Myrddin said, "is what we'll learn as we go along."

Graham rubbed his forehead as if he had a headache. "As we go along to *where*? Do you have any idea how ridiculous this sounds?"

Myrddin nodded. "I do. I've spent most of my life being called ridiculous."

"That's not what I mean," Graham said as he stood up. "I don't have time for this nonsense. I have a church to save."

"Reverend Ridley — " Malcolm said.

"Graham."

"*Graham*, would you mind if we went to see your church?" Malcolm asked.

"I don't mind at all. Why?"

He answered, "It might help us *all* if we saw it. Particularly now that we know it's where this whole adventure began."

29

I II III IV V VI VII VIII IX X XI XII

In his room at Ponsonby's, Adrian was stretched out on his bed with his arms tucked behind his head. He'd been staring at the ceiling for more than an hour. He didn't know what else to do while the war of his feelings raged inside of his head and heart. He was angry at himself, angry with Ponsonby, guilt-stricken and embarrassed.

Did I imagine our deal or did Ponsonby dupe me? he wondered. *Was I played for a fool?*

But did the answer really matter? Deal or dupe, friend or fool, either way his father had been betrayed at Adrian's hand. He had played Judas well, except he didn't do it for thirty pieces of silver, he did it for ...

For what? What was he really thinking when he blabbed to Ponsonby what he knew about the church's condition? If not thirty pieces of silver, what was he after? Security? Peace of mind? A hope for his future? A way to get back at his father's weakness?

Probably all of the above, he thought. Ponsonby was everything his father wasn't: strong, determined, successful. He was charming and beguiling. He taught Adrian the ways of the world — rather, *his* world — a world of money and cars and dreams that you could actually wrap your hands around and put in your pocket. It was a world where you could be the bully rather than bullied. It was a world where you were the master of the game rather than just a pawn who could be manipulated by those more cunning and powerful than you. That was Ponsonby's world and it was awfully attractive. After a lifetime of watching his father play servant, washing other men's feet, it was refreshing to believe in an alternative. But … was that really what Adrian believed?

What do you believe in? Who do you believe in? Those were the questions Ponsonby demanded Adrian to answer.

He suddenly sat up and swung his legs off the bed. His foot kicked what was left of the daily paper on the floor. Adrian looked down and nudged it with his toe. As it moved, his eye caught a glimpse of the small paragraph about King Arthur's arrival in England. He and Lewis had laughed when they read it earlier on their way back from York.

But now, for a moment, he wished it was true. He wished he could believe in things like that again. He wished it now. For if he could believe in a world where the unexplainable happened, then maybe he could believe in his father's world rather than Ponsonby's. What kind of meaning does money have in a world of miracles?

What do you believe in?

He stood up and walked to the window. He yanked the curtain aside and looked out into the fading day. The rain had stopped, the clouds from that afternoon moving on to other places, allowing the sun its time to shine before dropping behind the horizon.

What's it going to be? he asked himself, willing himself to make up his mind. Did he believe in his father's way or Ponsonby's way? Was he set to be a faithful push-over like his dad or a cynical non-believer like Ponsonby?

One way or another he had to decide. He couldn't stay in this limbo of indecision forever. Ponsonby would demand his loyalty further if he planned to stay at the manor. And, if his mother's tone on the phone was an indicator, he couldn't go home unless he was prepared to apologize and commit in some small way to respecting his father.

He had to decide what he believed.

And then he had to *do* something about it.

The five men crowded into Malcolm's rental car and drove to Christ Church. Graham was dismayed to see Ponsonby's Land Rover parked in the lot. *A vulture checking out the carcass*, he thought.

As they each unfolded themselves out of the small car, Ponsonby and a balding, spectacled man emerged from the church.

"Ah! Reverend Ridley." Ponsonby flashed his dazzling smile. "Glad you're here."

Graham was working on a snappy retort when Arthur, who had just climbed out of the car, suddenly roared and charged at Ponsonby. A confused cry went up from the four men who instantly chased after him.

"Good heavens!" Ponsonby exclaimed and ducked behind his companion, who looked stricken. Arthur grabbed Ponsonby's companion with one hand and tossed him aside like a rag doll. He then lunged at Ponsonby, who had the good sense and quick skill to jump in the other direction. Arthur narrowly missed him.

"What's this all about?" Ponsonby shouted.

By this time, Graham, Malcolm, and Jeff formed a tentative wall between Arthur and Ponsonby while Myrddin grabbed Arthur. He put his face close to Arthur's. "What are you doing, sire? Why are you attacking this man?"

"Do you not know him? Has he bewitched you? It is Mordred!"

"No, sire, no," Myrddin said. "You are mistaken."

"He has followed me into this dream! He has come to slay me!" Arthur said, then shouted at Ponsonby, "I know your wicked ways, vile betrayer! Stand and fight!"

"Sire, please," Myrddin pleaded. With great effort, he guided Arthur around the corner of the church. Their voices, arguing in Latin, could be heard after they were out of sight.

"What on earth is the matter with the man?" Ponsonby scowled.

Jeff helped the balding man to his feet. "Are you all right?"

"The name's Clydesdale and, no, I am not all right. Lunatics like that should be put away." Clydesdale sniffed as he dusted himself off.

"Sorry." Jeff retrieved his glasses from the ground and handed them over.

"Is this your way of dealing with your problems?" Ponsonby asked Graham. "Bring in a team of ruffians?"

"Obviously, he thought you were someone else," Graham replied, then asked, "Why are you here?"

"Clydesdale and I were looking over the grounds for . . . future planning."

Graham folded his arms. "Aren't you premature in making any plans?"

"Am I?"

"I've been given three days to come up with the money for renovations," Graham said.

Ponsonby laughed. "You don't really believe you can accomplish that kind of fund-raising in such a short amount of time."

Graham grinned. "Stranger things have happened."

"I'm Ponsonby," he said by way of introduction to Malcolm and Jeff, and Malcolm and Jeff introduced themselves as well.

"Malcolm Dubbs bought the oldest section of the church,"

Graham said dryly. "Would you like to send some inspectors over to have it condemned?"

Ponsonby grinned without amusement. "I'm sure even America has its own inspectors." He abruptly signaled to Clydesdale and they walked toward the Land Rover. "It's been *interesting* meeting you." He gestured toward Arthur. "And I suggest you put Chewbacca on a leash."

After Ponsonby and Clydesdale drove off, Graham, Malcolm, and Jeff walked around the church in the same direction Myrddin and Arthur had gone.

"They must be around where *your* ruin was," Graham said. His voice was tense, though he didn't know if it was because of the confrontation with Ponsonby or because he resented Malcolm for having part of his church in America.

Arthur was sitting on a large stone with a defiant expression as Myrddin paced in front of him. They were in a heated argument, which they cut off as soon as the others joined them.

"Problems?" Graham asked wryly.

Myrddin threw his hands up. "He's being unreasonable."

"It's nice to know we weren't the only ones who couldn't control him," Jeff said with a chuckle.

"He has it all wrong," Myrddin went on. "He thinks he's here to defeat Ponsonby."

Graham said, "He gets my vote for that."

"He thinks Ponsonby is Mordred, whom he believes somehow followed him into this time for their final battle," Myrddin explained irritably.

"If you're going to pretend that he's King Arthur, then why not pretend that Ponsonby is Mordred? Let them have it out to the bitter end," Graham suggested.

Myrddin frowned at Graham.

"Gentleman," Graham said, bowing politely, "this is where I say good evening. I can't imagine what you're going to do now, but I hope your Arthurian romance ends the way you want it to end. Perhaps you'll have some swash-buckling derring-do or save a damsel in distress. Better still, the prime minister might invite you 'round for tea at Number Ten to hear about Arthur's great mission. I look forward to reading all about it in the tabloids." Graham walked off toward his house.

Myrddin watched him go, then turned to the remaining three men. "He isn't normally like this. He's a changed man since this whole church business started."

"I don't blame him," Malcolm offered. "Everything that's happened *is* pretty far-fetched. And he brought up a valid point."

"What point?" Jeff asked.

"What *are* we supposed to do now?"

Inside the Land Rover as it bounced toward the manor house, Clydesdale said, "What do you suppose Ridley is up to?"

"I have no idea," Ponsonby said as he rounded a corner too fast. "Clydesdale, can you speak Latin?"

"No."

Ponsonby grunted. "I do."

31

The four men returned to the inn, where Malcolm arranged for supper to be brought to a small lounge in the back where they could talk in private. After they'd eaten, Jeff's attention fell to a television set on a table in the corner.

"Bored?" Malcolm asked him.

Jeff smiled, but didn't answer.

Then Malcolm, Myrddin, and Arthur pulled out various maps and spread them on the table. Malcolm was sure that part of the mystery about Arthur and his mission was connected to where he was *before* he came to the present.

"I believe his mission will reveal itself to us," Myrddin proclaimed. "We don't have to search for it."

"Maybe you're right," Malcolm said. "Or maybe we have a part to play in how it's revealed. Please ask Arthur to show us what he can on the maps."

Myrddin was skeptical, but translated into Latin anyway. "Can you look at this map and tell us where you were when you fell asleep?"

Arthur pointed at an area called Salisbury Plain and replied in Latin with Myrddin translating. "We gathered our armies here." He rifled through several of Malcolm's maps until he found one of the Glastonbury area. "Where are we now?"

Myrddin pointed to the area where the inn was situated.

"The church?"

Myrddin ran his finger along the paper and stopped at the small symbol of the cross indicating the church.

Malcolm tugged at his ear thoughtfully. "Why would he fall asleep in his tent on Salisbury Plain, but wind up in a church ruin in Fawlt Line? I know you summoned him with the horn, but — "

"Yes, I've been doing that faithfully for years."

"You mean you've been going up to the tower and blowing the horn *every* night?" Jeff asked in wonder.

"Not every night. On holy days, mostly."

"But why?"

"Because I believed he would come."

"But he came to the church ruin in America," Malcolm said. "Why?"

"I thought you already established the connection between the church ruin in Fawlt Line and the church in Wellsbridge," Myrddin said.

Arthur pointed to the map again. "Pray tell, what is meant by this symbol?"

"It's a symbol for a manor house, sire."

"Manor house?"

"Yes. In this case, it belongs to Mr. Ponsonby," Myrddin told him.

Arthur nodded and put the map away.

Malcolm continued, "We established the connection between my church ruin and Christ Church, that's true. Maybe Arthur showed up there because that's where the ruin was. Which means that he was *supposed* to show up here in Wellsbridge."

"A worthy consideration," Myrddin nodded.

"But why the church at Wellsbridge at all? Why not wake up at the Abbey ruin in Glastonbury or Cadbury or any of the sites more generally acknowledged as places connected with Arthur?" Malcolm asked.

Myrddin's face lit up. "Perhaps Arthur wasn't buried in Glastonbury after all, as the legends say. Perhaps his body *was* carried away by the Lady of the Lake to another place nearby — to Wellsbridge, which also would have been an island at the time. Perhaps everyone has had it all wrong by a couple of miles."

"Do you really believe a lady of a lake carried him away in a boat?" Jeff asked from his place in front of the television.

"Do *you* really believe that King Arthur is standing here in front of you right now?"

Jeff got Malcolm's point and returned to flipping channels.

Arthur announced that he was tired and wanted to go to sleep. Myrddin translated and Malcolm took him up one floor to the room they'd booked for him. It adjoined Malcolm's room. He began to explain where everything was, but Arthur seemed impatient to be left alone. Malcolm obliged him.

Myrddin was beside himself when Malcolm returned to the lounge. "I must telephone Graham!"

"Why? He doesn't seem interested."

"He will now. This bit of information could help him!"

Malcolm didn't get it. "Information about what?"

"His church. It may be the miracle he's been looking for. Establishing the church's connection to Arthur could save it as an historical landmark!"

✿ ✿ ✿

"Who will believe it?" Graham asked in a sour voice from the other end of the line. Since the lounge wasn't equipped with a telephone, Myrddin had phoned Graham from a payphone in the front lobby of the inn.

"Why wouldn't they?" Myrddin asked.

Graham chuckled. "Oh, I see. They're going to take *your* word for it, right? How about the *Americans*? Those are credible sources for British history. Or perhaps you could set up an interview with Arthur and *he'll* tell everyone how the lady of the lake took him to my church after he died?"

"Graham — "

"No. We're still stuck, Myrddin."

"Don't let this defeat you, Graham," Myrddin said. "Good will come from this. Somehow it all fits together — in a way only God knows."

"Thanks for phoning, Myrddin," Graham replied as if he hadn't heard a word the old sage said.

"Good-night."

They hung up.

Myrddin walked back to the lounge. Arthur's return was important for the entire nation, there was no doubt about that, and yet somehow his return seemed more directly related to the events surrounding Christ Church and Graham Ridley. It was all connected somehow, but even Myrddin was perplexed as to how.

Good will come from this, Myrddin had said. He believed it wholeheartedly.

Perhaps the mission was to get *Graham* to believe it.

○ ○ ○

"Why do you have only five television channels in this country?" Jeff asked Myrddin. "It's pretty boring."

"Some hotels carry satellite channels, though you'd find them boring as well."

"Why?"

"They carry mostly American programs," Myrddin said with a smile. "Where is Malcolm?"

Jeff hooked a thumb toward the staircase. "In his room."

"Of course," Myrddin said, suddenly realizing how late it was. "I suppose I should go home now."

He turned to go, then decided to peek in on Arthur. Ascending the stairs, he went to the room. He tapped lightly on the door, but no one answered. *Could the man be asleep?* he wondered. He tried the handle and it turned easily. The room was dark and silent. A breeze swept through the room and Myrddin realized the window was open.

"Your Highness?" Myriddin whispered toward the bed in the shadows.

Malcolm stepped into the light of the doorway, wiping his face with a towel. "I thought I heard someone knocking." He squinted into the darkness. "Where's Arthur?"

Myrddin fumbled for a light switch and pushed it. A light came on next to the bed. The bed was empty. Curtains blllowed gently next to the open window. Arthur was gone.

32

I II III IV V VI VII VIII IX X XI XII

Unable to sleep, Graham said good-night to his wife and took a walk across the field between his house and Christ Church. It soothed and calmed him to hear the swish of his feet against the damp grass. The occasional hoot of an owl or childlike cry of foxes in the nearby woods helped to remind him that an entirely different world existed and went about its business, untouched by his troubles.

Graham looked up at the blinking stars. Was there somebody up in that vastness who actually cared about Graham's life?

In the deepest part of his heart, Graham hoped so. *His ways are not our ways*, a writer in the Bible had said. How can we possibly hope to understand him?

Graham had no idea how all of the pieces would fall into place. But, for just a moment, walking in that field toward the church, Graham dared to hope that Myrddin might be right. Maybe the pieces would fit together miraculously and everything *would* turn out all right in the end.

His thoughts became a small prayer. *God*, he said, *I wish you would do something, say something, that might serve as a sign that you really are in the middle of this mess and not asleep somewhere.*

Graham stopped in his tracks and waited like an expectant child. The night was still.

Except for the unmistakable sound from the church of stone scraping against stone.

Graham's heart lurched at the thought of a vandal or, more likely, one of Ponsonby's men wreaking damage on the church just to ensure its demise. He chased the sound, slowing down when he came to the corner of the church where the ruin had been. He peered around as quietly as he could.

Arthur, if that's who he really was, was busy moving several large stones away from the church wall. That, in and of itself, was unusual enough. What made it more so was that he was dressed in a long cape. Under the cape he wore a long tunic with the symbol of a red dragon stitched to the front. His waist was bound by a gold belt, his legs were covered with brown tights, and on his feet were leather shoes.

As Graham watched, Arthur reached into the cavity he'd created by moving the stones. He retrieved something that, for a moment, was out of Graham's line of sight. His arms and shoulders went taut from the weight of it. Graham was almost certain he heard a low pulsating hum.

Arthur turned fully into Graham's view and held in both hands a sword in a golden scabbard. Graham watched in awe as Arthur pulled the sword free from its casing. Even in the starlight, it shone like it was lit from the inside-out. Jewels sparkled on the handle. The silver blade danced and dazzled as Arthur tested it against an invisible opponent. It was beautiful. It was majestic. It was ...

Excalibur, Graham thought. He immediately rebuked himself for thinking it. It couldn't be Excalibur, he reminded himself, because this man wasn't Arthur. He *couldn't* be. *Even if he looked exactly like he'd always imagined Arthur would look: it was impossible.*

Or was it?

Holding the sword by the handle, Arthur pointed it downward at arm's length and plunged it into the grassy ground. He knelt

next to it, performed the sign of the cross and prayed for a moment. After that, he stood up again and carefully put the sword
back into the scabbard and attached it to his belt. Grabbing his
bundle of modern clothes, he tossed them into the hole, then
strode purposefully away from the church.

Graham leaned against the cold stone wall. His practical,
gotta-get-up-in-the-morning sensibilities told him to go to bed
and forget what he'd just seen. His childlike self told him to follow
along to see what the man was going to do next.

What if he really is King Arthur? the inner-child teased him.

Graham took a deep breath and cautiously slid from the wall
to follow.

33

I II III IV V VI VII VIII IX X XI XII

Adrian made a decision.

He looked out of his window, his gaze moving from the dark field to the splash of light on the patio outside of Ponsonby's study. Adrian gritted his teeth with determination and was about to turn toward his bedroom door when, out of the corner of his eye, he saw something move in the shadows near the study windows. It prowled along the wall and entered into the light for only a moment. Adrian's eyes bulged at the sight. It was a man dressed in ancient clothes carrying a gigantic sword.

King Arthur? No, it couldn't be.

The figure disappeared into the shadows again.

Adrian stepped back from the window, puzzled by what he had seen. *An intruder — a dangerous intruder!* Worried for Ponsonby's safety, he raced from his room and down a servant's stairway to the door leading outside from the kitchen. Most of the help would have settled in for the night, he knew. He paused, unsure of what to do. Should he raise an alarm that would also alert the intruder, or watch him closely and then quietly phone the police?

He decided on the latter and slipped out from the kitchen to a small porch. Moving as silently as he could, he hugged the wall until he got to a corner leading around to the patio itself. He slowly peeked around the corner.

In a quick one-two action, a hand grabbed Adrian's shirt while another pressed hard against his mouth.

"Sssshhhh," the owner of the hands hissed.

Adrian looked into the eyes of his father. "MMMmmmphhh!" he exclaimed.

"Be quiet, will you?" Graham whispered into his ear, then took his hand from the boy's mouth.

"What are you doing here? Are you trying to get arrested?" Adrian whispered back to him.

"I think I'm sleepwalking," Graham answered.

"What?" Adrian leaned away to see if his father had lost his mind and dressed up like King Arthur. He hadn't. He was in a sweatshirt, jeans, and sneakers. Adrian was relieved. "Dad, why are you here?"

"Why are *you* here?" was Graham's retort. "Are you out strolling the grounds or, as Ponsonby's henchman have you come out to protect him from prowlers carrying large swords?"

"I saw him from the window. Who is it — what's he doing?"

"I followed him from the church to find out," Graham said. "But I've lost him."

They looked around, but couldn't see Arthur. Finally, Graham said, "Dad we have to talk."

Graham agreed. "Maybe after we find our King Arthur. We can't let him run loose around the grounds — not with that sword. Now which way do you suggest we go?"

Adrian looked around. "To the other side of the patio. That's the direction he was headed when I saw him from my window."

"Lead on, MacDuff," Graham said.

The two of them crept across the patio toward the light spilling out from the study. Adrian heard voices through one of the open windows and stopped to look. Beyond the thin white curtains, he saw two men walk into the study.

Graham came up alongside him and whispered. "Ponsonby and Clydesdale?"

Adrian nodded. "What are they up to at this time of night?"

"Don't you know?" Graham asked sarcastically. "I thought you were in his fullest confidence."

Adrian ignored the comment and moved closer to the window. Graham followed him. Clydesdale had stopped at the edge of the desk while Ponsonby went around and clicked for a moment on his computer keyboard. "All in all a good day's work," Ponsonby said.

"As soon as you transfer the money into the proper accounts, we'll get the rest of it sorted out," Clydesdale said. "They're anxious to put it to an end, particularly the council members."

"I have it all here," Ponsonby told him as he tapped his computer screen. "Tell them to relax. There's no opposition. Ridley can't do a thing. He's a wet fish who wouldn't know how to start a fight, let alone win one."

"I resent that," Graham whispered in protest.

"Well, it's true," Adrian said.

Graham growled, "Oh, and I suppose you think that fighting the way Ponsonby fights is the way to win?"

"Ssshhh," Adrian hissed, his attention still on the proceedings inside.

"It's done," Ponsonby said after typing away at his computer for a few minutes.

Clydesdale adjusted his glasses. "In that case, I'll go home now. I want to be at their offices bright and early tomorrow."

"You do that." Ponsonby grinned and walked with him to the hall. "Rest assured you'll have a bonus on the other end of this as well."

The two men disappeared into the hall and Adrian guessed Ponsonby was walking Clydesdale to the front door. "Quick, give me a leg up," Adrian said.

"What?"

"I want to have a look at that screen." Adrian began scaling the wall to the window even without his father's help.

"You *live* here, remember?" Graham said.

Adrian hooked his arms on the sill and pulled himself into the study. "He never lets me near his computer unless he's there. I think he's paying people off, Dad."

Against his better judgment, Graham gave Adrian a hard lift through the window. Adrian hit the floor with a thump then scrambled to the computer.

Graham watched anxiously from the patio as Adrian scrolled up and down the screen, then slowly and as softly as possible punched the keys on the keyboard. There were voices in the hall. Graham's heart jumped to his throat. "Come out of there, son," Graham whispered harshly.

"Just a minute," Adrian whispered in reply, and seemed to spy something that he reached for and retrieved. "Go around to the front door and stall him," Adrian said.

"Stall him?"

"Tell him you want to talk about the church — anything — "

Graham hesitated, unsure, and then rushed into the darkness, heading for the front of the house.

The door opened and Ponsonby walked into his study.

34

I II III IV V VI VII VIII IX X XI XII

"He was here," Myrddin said after investigating the side of Christ Church where the ruins had been. Malcolm and Jeff were with him.

"What makes you so sure?"

Myrddin pulled Arthur's modern clothes from the hole in the stones.

"I hope he's not running around naked somewhere," Malcolm said.

"No, he's dressed." Myrddin scouted around the area. The headlights of Malcolm's car made his bony shadow bounce on the church wall.

Malcolm was puzzled. "Why did he come here?"

"To get his clothes," Jeff answered abruptly. "And Excalibur!"

Malcolm looked astonished. "Of course. This is where they went from the church ruin in Fawlt Line. I should've known."

Myrddin stalked around nervously. "If he has Excalibur, then I know where he's gone."

"Where?" Malcolm and Jeff asked together.

"Ponsonby's."

"Why there?"

"Arthur's certain that Ponsonby is Mordred," Myrddin said.

"But he's *not*."

"It doesn't matter," Myrddin explained. "You have to see things the way Arthur sees them. The people of his day were steeped in the power of *symbols*, not logic. Forces were at work then that we don't understand now, and often they were captured in symbols. The Cross of Christ symbolized sacrifice, goodness, and redemption. Excalibur symbolized power and authority. The Grail symbolized God's blessing on Britain. Even the king himself symbolized purity of heart and virtue. Mordred symbolized corruption, ruthless ambition, and evil."

"But that was Mordred a long time ago," Jeff stated. "What does Arthur think he can do to Ponsonby now?"

"He said today that if Britain is in a spiritual crisis, then Mordred and his kind are the cause. From his experience, there's only one way to deal with such men. *Kill them.*"

"Let's go," Malcolm said. The three men hurried to the car.

Adrian hadn't seen Ponsonby's fury until then, but it was cold and brittle and poured icy sweat all over him even in that cozy study.

"What do you think you're doing?" Ponsonby demanded, but the answer was all too obvious.

Adrian stood frozen in front of the computer.

Ponsonby scowled. "This is unfortunate. I was prepared to train you, to be your mentor, you know . . ."

The room was silent except for the click in Adrian's throat when he swallowed.

Ponsonby closed the study door then slowly crossed the room toward the desk. "Do you have any idea how many men would like to know what I know — who'd beg to learn from me? You had the chance. But you've blown it, Adrian. I asked you to make a choice and, like your father, you made the wrong choice."

"Is it the wrong choice?" Adrian said in a thin voice.

"You're trembling, like him," Ponsonby said with a laugh.

"Maybe that's because I *am* like him," Adrian said defiantly. "I'll take his love and his faith over your cruel life and heartless *car* collection any day!"

Somehow it didn't come out as grand as he'd hoped, but the meaning was clear.

Ponsonby was at the edge of the desk now. "You have your

father's way with words, too." With surprising speed, Ponsonby grabbed Adrian by the arm and dragged him to a large chair near the desk. He pushed him into it.

"What are you going to do? You can't keep me here. You can't do anything to me," Adrian said, wanting to believe it.

"Well, now, let's consider our options," Ponsonby said. "I suppose I could have you arrested for breaking and entering, stealing valuable goods ..." He raised his finger as if he'd thought of a good idea. "That one has potential. You could be knocked unconscious in the Antiques Display Room as if I'd caught you there trying to steal my Ming vase."

The thought of being knocked unconscious by Ponsonby in *any* room didn't appeal to Adrian. *Where are you, Dad?* he wondered.

Ponsonby brightened. "Come to think of it, the scandal of Reverend Ridley's son being arrested for theft will make my job a lot easier. Thank you, Adrian, you have your father's knack for being useful in all the wrong ways."

The door bell rang, followed by relentless pounding.

Ponsonby turned to his desk and hit the talk button on the small intercom. "Leave it! No one answer that door!" he shouted to the servants. "It's an intruder! Call the police!"

Ponsonby chuckled as he turned to face Adrian again. He was startled to find Adrian out of the chair. He was even more startled to get socked in the jaw by the boy.

Burning pain shot through Adrian's hand, wrist, and arm.

Ponsonby was pushed back by the punch, but returned quickly, slugging Adrian in the stomach.

Adrian doubled over and fell to the floor.

"You're a pest, do you know that?" Ponsonby grabbed Adrian and yanked his head back. He drew his arm back to throw another punch when the windows suddenly exploded inward.

Startled, Ponsonby swung around, allowing Adrian to fall to the floor. Shards of glass flew in every direction as King Arthur used his sword to hack away at the panes, sills, and frames. Once it was clear, he then hoisted himself in one swift move into the study.

"You again," Ponsonby growled, annoyed.

Adrian, who had learned a little Latin at school, thought he heard Arthur shout, "Look well to yourself!" He lifted up Excalibur in an attack stance. "I will have thee this night and will thwart your evildoings on this land and the evil thou wouldst do to me in battle tomorrow."

"You're a lunatic," Ponsonby shouted back at him in Latin, then said in English, "Who do you think you are in that ridiculous costume?"

"Thou art villain and traitor both," Arthur said. "Prepare to die."

"I was a master swordsman at Cambridge. I have no intention of dying," Ponsonby said, then spun around toward the fireplace and grabbed one of the crossed swords hanging above it. He brought it around with a crash against Excalibur.

I II III IV V VI VII VIII IX X XI XII

Clutching his stomach, Adrian crawled out of harm's way behind a chair and watched the sword fight with open-mouthed fascination. Arthur and Ponsonby rained powerful blows on each other and thrust and parried with remarkable skill. Adrian felt that he'd been transported to another time to witness a fierce battle between two old enemies. The men's grunts and loud *chings!* of steel on steel brought the servants to the study door, but Ponsonby had locked it and all they could do was stand outside and pound loudly. The clamor seemed to add to the intensity of the fight as the two men sped up their thrusts and defenses. They crashed into the furniture and slashed the decorations on every flat surface, including the walls.

Graham appeared at the window and called out, "Adrian! Son! Are you all right?"

Adrian signaled he was, then shouted, "Stay back! Don't try to come in or you'll get hurt."

Arthur, who didn't have the benefit of being a master swordsman at any university, was the stronger and more determined fighter. He drove Ponsonby into the corner of the room and hit the man's sword relentlessly with one blow after another. Ponsonby resisted as much as he could, but his strength was no match for Arthur's and he went down on his knees. Then with a flick of

Excalibur, Arthur knocked Ponsonby's sword out of his hands, then aimed the tip at Ponsonby's neck.

"Have mercy on me," Ponsonby pleaded in Latin. His face was pallid and drenched in sweat. "I'll do whatever you ask."

The door of the study was finally opened by Walters, a wary butler, but he and the servants behind him froze where they were. A lone voice barked to "get out of the way" and Myrddin pushed his way through the small crowd with Malcolm and Jeff.

"Stop!" Malcolm called out in Latin.

"King Arthur!" Myrddin said with great command as he entered the room.

Arthur respectfully turned to him.

"This is not the way! It wasn't in your time, nor in ours," he appealed. "Ponsonby and his kind will only be defeated by the faithful — men and women of true character whose hopes are set on the things beyond this life."

Arthur looked from Myrddin to Ponsonby and back at Myrddin again.

"In all of your years as king, did you ever find that the sword brought anything but pain and misery?"

The question went unanswered by Arthur.

Myrddin went on, "This isn't why you are here, sire. Not for murder."

Arthur leveled his gaze on Ponsonby and then tapped the quivering man's chin with the flat of his blade. "Confess your treachery against God and man," Arthur demanded.

Ponsonby stammered.

"Confess!" Arthur shouted, the blade again in position to do great harm.

"I confess," said Ponsonby.

"Give half of your lands and wealth to the poor," Arthur added.

Ponsonby paused and lowered his head.

"Speak, traitor."

"I agree," Ponsonby said.

"Restore the church."

Ponsonby nodded. "Done."

Arthur stepped away and replaced Excalibur in its scabbard. No sooner had he done this than there was another commotion at the door. Three policemen arrived, and one immediately rushed to Ponsonby. "You all right, Mr. Ponsonby?"

Ponsonby stood up. "Of course I'm not all right. Do I look all right? Does this *room* look all right? I want you to arrest that madman for breaking and entering, destroying private property, assault and battery ... "

The three constables turned to Arthur, who knew in any language that Ponsonby had gone back on his word.

"Throw the sword to the floor, sir," one of the constables said as the three slowly approached him.

"What has the liar done? What do they want?" Arthur asked Myrddin.

Myrddin glared at Ponsonby, then frowned at Arthur. "They want to take you to prison."

Ponsonby laughed derisively. "That's right. King Arthur in prison. I'll have to get pictures."

The constables closed in on Arthur, whose eyes darted around. Suddenly he pushed the policemen aside and in a few giant steps left the way he'd come in: through the window.

The police shouted and gave chase, scrambling as best they could through the remnants of the shattered frame.

Adrian looked for his father, but couldn't see him. Then a hand was on his collar and before he knew what was happening he was being pulled by Malcolm and Jeff through the crowd of servants — who pressed forward to help their master. They raced down the hall and out the front door.

" 'Give me a leg up,' you said. And I did! What was I thinking?" Graham's voice echoed off of the walls and stained glass windows of Christ Church as he marched back and forth in front of the first pew where Adrian was seated. The only other sound in the church was a faint creaking coming from one of the doors.

Malcolm and Jeff sat mutely in other pews nearby — this seemed like a family matter. Arthur sat dejectedly next to the altar, an odd table made of stone, with his head lowered into his arms. Myrddin paced thoughtfully next to a nearby pillar.

"None of this would've happened if I'd dragged you home right then and there," Graham said.

"Don't be so certain," Myrddin corrected him. "These events may have been set into motion regardless."

"Here we go again," Graham groaned, then looked out at the empty church. Something caught his eye.

"I *had* to see what was on the computer," Adrian said. "It was my only chance to . . . to undo the damage I've done."

"Which damage in particular?" Graham asked.

Adrian hesitated, then decided to throw all of his cards on the table. "The inspection of the church. I was the one who told him about the foundation."

If silence itself could echo, it would have at that moment.

Adrian hung his head. He didn't expect this scene to be

played out in front of so many strangers. He braced himself for his father's anger.

Graham knelt next to the pew and faced him directly. "Why?"

"I was confused. I thought … it would free you," Adrian said. "I thought that if you lost this church and Ponsonby made the archdeacon send us somewhere else that you'd — we'd — be happier. I was sick and tired of people like Ponsonby and the archdeacon bullying you around. I got it all wrong. I'm sorry."

"Did you hear that, Anne?" Graham suddenly called out.

Everyone looked around, confused. Anne walked down the aisle. She was the reason a door had creaked. "I heard," she said as she arrived at the front pew.

Adrian looked helplessly at his parents. "I feel awful. This is my fault." He dropped his face onto his folded arms.

Anne lightly stroked the back of her son's neck. "It's all right, Adrian. We all make the wrong choices sometimes."

Graham leaned close to Adrian's covered face. "I'm sorry too. I should have given you a better reason to respect me, and I didn't."

Adrian lifted his head. The three of them looked at each other and volumes of unspoken words passed between them.

Graham chuckled. "Well, Myrddin, you said there would be a miracle when Arthur came and here it is."

"Let's hope this atmosphere of forgiveness goes on after they arrest us all," Myrddin said.

"Arrest us!" Jeff exclaimed.

"Don't think Ponsonby is going to forget about what happened. He'll come back at us somehow — with charges of burglary or assault — anything he can come up with," Myrddin said.

Arthur entreated Myrddin to translate what was being said. After Myrddin did, Arthur suddenly slapped his hand against the marble floor that made up part of the altar area and spoke in Latin.

Myrddin turned to the rest and said in English, "He thinks it's his fault. He failed."

"If I could figure out what in the world was going on, I'd say we *all* failed," Malcolm said.

"Is this some sort of therapy group?" Anne asked.

Arthur continued with a deep sadness in his voice, "In the past and in the present, I chose wrongly. The glory of Camelot was always overshadowed by my failures."

Myrddin translated, then sat down next to Arthur and patted his arm. "You're right, of course."

Arthur looked at him, surprised.

"It's the folly of every king," Myrddin went on. "You failed only when you pursued your own prideful heart, vanity, and glory — and not the glory of God."

"You speak truth, old sage. Only now after all these years can I see it," he said mournfully.

"Perhaps that's why you're here, sire — to learn this lesson before your battle against Mordred — so that when you face him, you face him not with your glory in mind, but *God's* glory," Myrddin suggested.

"It is my *final* battle, if thy stories are correct," Arthur reminded him.

Myrddin smiled wearily. "Is it ever too late to learn a lesson as important as that? Down to our last battle, our last minute, our last breath, it is worth remembering. The glory of Camelot fades just as all man-made glory fades, but the glory of God transcends this life and goes on forever."

Arthur unhooked Excalibur from his belt and laid it next to Myrddin. "Thy wisdom is great, as always. I must face the evil of Mordred on the battlefield in my own time — not here in this dream. Not by the power of the sword, but by God's power alone. God's will be done."

"Translation please?" Graham asked.

Myrddin relayed the conversation to the group, then stood up before them, like a wizened preacher now in his pulpit. "It's a lesson for all of us. We've been striving so hard to save this church: playing power games as if they matter at all. The future of this *physical* church shouldn't be our primary concern — it's a glory that fades. The *spiritual* future of our nation is far more important and will never fade so long as it burns bright in the hearts of true believers. *What do you believe, Graham?*" he suddenly asked. "Do you believe that you are called by God to preach, to be a minister in his church, and do you believe that Ponsonby or an archdeacon can stop you from that calling? No. They may stop your *career*, but since when is God's calling in your life a career? If you believe in God's calling, then you can't be stopped. *What do you believe?* Do you believe in miracles?"

Graham hung his head. "I'm beginning to ... again."

"Do you now believe that this man is King Arthur?"

Graham blushed. "I'm willing to concede that, yes, he might be King Arthur. Though it's beyond me why I would think so."

"Might be! Beyond you!" Myrddin cried, his face shining and his voice booming against the windows. "What is it you want, Graham? What do you expect?"

Graham stammered a non-answer.

Myrddin's gaze fell on each person in the church. "This is why King Arthur has returned. To ask the hearts of his countrymen what it is they truly believe about God and his place in this world. Is it a miracle you want? Is it? Then behold a miracle!"

Suddenly the doors to the church flew inward and police officers poured in. Some wore body armor and carried machine guns. Ponsonby marched in last, at the side of a man with a round body and ruddy, Dickensian face.

"I'm Police Inspector Cassidy. Nobody move," the ruddy-faced man shouted.

Arthur instinctively leapt to his feet with Excalibur in hand.

"Shoot him if he moves even an inch," Ponsonby said. The sight of Ponsonby made Arthur roar with anger.

Myrddin stepped in front of him and in a tone that sharply contrasted the commotion around them, he said simply, "Remember the lesson. Put away the sword. This is not why you've come. The day will be won by miracles, not might."

Arthur growled then, to their amazement, cried out in English, "God grant me the strength for *this* miracle!"

With both hands, he raised the sword upside-down and thrust its point into the stone altar. With a starburst of sparks, the blade went deeper and deeper — a hum and metallic ringing assailing everyone's ears. Waves of light pulsed away from the altar and in the light they each saw the tired and dark stone walls of the church ablaze and bright as if newly built. The woodwork on the pews, choir stalls, and pulpits — dried and scarred from years of use — appeared recently polished, the rich brown a contrast to the ornate gold of the crosses, candlesticks, and insignias that only now seemed to light up all around them. The stained-glass windows were aglow, the colors vivid, and the scenes of Jesus came to life before their eyes.

With a decisive thump, the sword's point struck the bottom. Only a few inches of the glowing blade could be seen between the top of the altar and the hilt. The light then disappeared and the church looked as it had been.

Arthur collapsed to his knees next to the stone altar, one hand still clinging to Excalibur's handle. He lowered his shaggy head and prayed.

"Behold your miracle," Myrddin said to the shaken crowd.

Graham, who had also fallen to his knees in that moment, noticed that some of the police had done the same. The rest looked at the sword silently, eyes wide, mouths agape.

"It's a magic trick," Ponsonby shouted, a tremor in his voice. He rushed to the altar and grabbed the hilt of the sword. "It's an illusion to throw us off," he announced and gave the sword a firm tug. It wouldn't budge. He took the hilt in both hands and pulled with all of his might, the veins standing out on his forehead, his neck looking as if it might explode. The sword would not yield.

Myrddin looked at Graham and Adrian, a smile on his worn face. "As I said: behold, your miracle."

Inspector Cassidy shuffled in his place, his mouth moving, his eyes searching the walls and windows of the church as if trying to confirm what he'd seen only a moment before.

"Do something!" Ponsonby commanded him.

"What, for instance?" Cassidy said with a croak.

"Arrest them!" Ponsonby snarled. "That's what you came to do, isn't it?"

"Oh — right," the inspector said. "Breaking and entering and assault I believe were the charges."

"I'd like to add one," Adrian said.

Cassidy was perplexed. "Would you, young man?"

"Yes, sir," Adrian replied, then pointed to Ponsonby. "I have proof that he's been bribing public officials to secure this land for his commercial schemes."

Ponsonby was livid. "He's lying! This deluded and ungrateful young man *thinks* he saw something incriminating on my computer at home. It's all a mistake and he certainly doesn't have any proof."

"That's quite an accusation," Cassidy said stiffly to Adrian.

Adrian reached into his shirt pocket and pulled out a thin, silver mini-drive. "All the evidence is on this. It's a complete record of Ponsonby's pay-offs, including a group of bank transfers made tonight."

"He's bluffing!" Ponsonby sneered. "He stole that drive from my office!"

Adrian shook his head. "How could I break in to a house where I was living? There's nothing illegal about that, is there, Inspector?"

Cassidy groaned. "This is getting awfully complicated, Ponsonby."

Suddenly there was a flash from the back of the church, then another, and another. Everyone spun around in the direction of the light. A photographer stood next to Andy Samuelson, the tabloid reporter who'd chased after Arthur at the airport. "Smile everybody," Samuelson said.

Another flash went off.

"Who are you?" Ponsonby demanded.

"Andy Samuelson with the *Sun*, or the *Star*, or maybe the *Times*, depending on who'll pay me the most for this story." He gestured to Malcolm and Jeff. "I've been chasing these Yanks all over the countryside to get some snaps of King Arthur. But now that I have some corruption and bribery to go with it, all the better!"

Ponsonby's face went crimson while Cassidy's went pale.

"I can see the headlines now. *Arthur returns to Britain to save church and expose corruption*!" Samuelson said gleefully, then to the photographer: "Get a few pictures of that sword in the stone. Front page stuff!"

Cassidy held up his hands. "That's it. Everybody comes to the police station. We'll sort this whole thing out down there!"

"I think I may want to call the American embassy," Malcolm said.

Cassidy grumbled something unintelligible and pushed his way to the door.

39

I II III IV V VI VII VIII IX X XI XII

A full-blown argument filled the halls and the small interrogation room at the Glastonbury Police Station.

"Even as evidence, it's not admissible. It was obtained by illegal means!" Ponsonby shouted at Cassidy.

Red faced, Cassidy shook the printout of the disc's contents at Ponsonby. "Admissible or not, I want an explanation of this!" The printout was a complete list with the names of city and county officials, and inspectors who'd been bribed, along with account numbers and substantial sums of money that had changed hands.

Three of the officials, who'd been dragged out of bed and now stood dazed and sleepy before Cassidy, jumped in to the argument simultaneously. "I don't know anything about this ... Where's my lawyer? ... I never took a single penny ..."

The shouts reached through the thick glass of the interrogation room to the waiting area, where the group from the church was sitting along with the reporter. Samuelson scribbled notes on a pad and laughed to himself. "Nothing like the sound of grown men covering their tracks."

"Will you really print this story?" Graham asked him.

Samuelson looked at Graham as if he'd just landed from another planet. "You better believe it. King Arthur, the church, the scandal ... classic tabloid journalism."

A door down the hall slammed, muffling the arguing voices. Cassidy's footsteps rang heavy as he pushed open the door and gazed at the crowd in the waiting room. "You're all free to go for tonight. But be here first thing tomorrow morning to answer some questions about what happened at Ponsonby's manor."

"Including him?" Myrddin asked, hooking a thumb toward Arthur.

Arthur, arms folded, leaned against the soda machine. The contrast of a man dressed for the fifth century against the red and white lights and buttons of a dispenser made for quite a picture.

"*Especially* him," Cassidy said. "If nothing else, I want to know how he pulled off that light show at the church."

"It was no show," said Myrddin. "It was a miracle."

From the interrogation room, it sounded like a chair had been thrown over. Cassidy groaned. "Back to the wrestling match," he said and stormed off.

"I want interviews with all of you," Samuelson announced as everyone stood to leave.

"Oh, please," Anne yawned. "We're going home now."

"I don't think we'll want that kind of press coverage," Graham said.

Samuelson said quickly, "It's to your advantage, you know. The more exposure there is for your church, the more interest there'll be in restoring it."

Graham considered the point. "You're right. Let's talk tomorrow."

"And just think of all the revenue that'll be generated by people who'll want to see the mysterious 'sword in the stone altar,'" Samuelson added.

The idea hadn't occurred to Graham, but he had to admit it was true.

"How about you Yanks? Care to give me an exclusive about your adventure with King Arthur?"

Malcolm and Jeff glanced at each other. "No comment," they said.

○ ○ ○

At their cars in front of the police station, a silence fell on the seven of them. Policemen and their suspects gawked openly at Arthur and his outfit. Arthur didn't seem to mind.

"You'll be staying in the area for a while, I assume," Graham said hopefully to Malcolm and Jeff.

"I think so. No point coming all this way and not visit for a while," Malcolm replied. "I'll want to return to the church."

"Come for tea," Anne said. "We'll expect you tomorrow at four."

"Delighted," Malcolm smiled, then turned to Adrian. "What about you, Adrian? Will you be there?"

Adrian looked sheepishly at his parents. "I don't know. Will I?"

"It's your choice," Graham said. "We'd be happy to have you home again."

"Then I'll be there," Adrian said.

"Good," Jeff responded. "Maybe you can show me what guys our age do for fun around here."

Graham put a hand lightly on Myrddin's shoulder. "I want to talk to you about all of this. There are things I don't understand."

Myrddin raised an eyebrow. "For example?"

"I thought you said the point wasn't to save Christ Church."

"Saving Christ Church *wasn't* the point," Myrddin affirmed. "But isn't it just like God to go ahead and save it anyway. That was *your* miracle."

Graham agreed. "We'll expect you and Arthur for tea as well, you old lunatic."

The Ridley family crawled into Graham's Mini and waved as they drove away.

Jeff yawned and stretched. "Well, I guess we should go back to the inn now, right?"

"I guess so." Malcolm took a few steps toward his car, then realized that Arthur and Myrddin weren't following.

Jeff said, "Myrddin?"

Myrddin and Arthur were deep in a whispered counsel. Myrddin nodded, then addressed Malcolm. "We have to go to my cottage, and then there's one more mission, if you're willing."

40

Dawn offered a ribbon of yellow, pink, and blue on the horizon as Malcolm pulled the car to a halt. Stretching out from the road, Salisbury Plain rose and fell in gentle slopes through a deep fog. The four men climbed out of the car.

Jeff shivered, having just awakened after falling asleep during the drive. "Okay, so what're we doing here?"

"Saying good-bye," Malcolm said.

"Good-bye! Who's leaving?"

Arthur looked wistfully at the field. He looked older now.

"Oh," Jeff said sadly. "But he never met the queen or the prime minister."

"He did what he came to do," Myrddin said. "Things have been set into motion now that will not be stopped."

A silence fell on them like dew on grass.

Abruptly, Arthur grabbed Malcolm's and Jeff's hands.

"God be with you," said Malcolm.

Jeff, startled, only managed to say, "See you later."

Arthur then embraced Myrddin and spoke gentle words in Latin. He brushed a tear away from his eye.

"I'll see you in my dreams," Myrddin said in English, then repeated it again in Latin as he winked at Arthur.

He turned his head suddenly as if he heard something out

on the field. He moved in that direction, then raised his hand in salute to Malcolm, Jeff, and Myrddin.

"*Vale: oremus semper,*" Arthur said on the edge of a sigh.

"Farewell: let us pray for one another always," Myrddin translated and waved back.

Jeff's expression was one of unmasked surprise.

"What's wrong?" Malcolm asked him.

"Those were the same words Elizabeth said in the church ruin at Fawlt Line."

As Arthur moved into the thick fog, Myrddin pulled a horn, curved like a ram's horn, out from under his coat. He lifted it to his lips and blew as hard as he could. The mournful sound echoed across the plain.

In the misty morning they saw a shimmer of light as the sun flashed on armor and sword. A host of mounted knights, pennants flying in a breeze, approached Arthur. He climbed onto his horse and, for a moment, they saw a marvelous king approaching his last battle. He turned and waved as the fog erased the vision from their sight. It was a dream.

"Or was it a dream?" Malcolm asked Myrddin as they drove back to Wellsbridge.

"A dream, perhaps. But whose dream? His or ours?" Myrddin said cryptically.

"Huh?" Jeff grunted from the back seat.

"Was Arthur a dream to us or were we in Arthur's dream?"

Jeff adjusted to a more comfortable position. "I'm too tired to think about it," he muttered. "I just wanna know what'll happen to Arthur without Excalibur. He left it here. Doesn't he need it for his last battle?"

"Yes. But now he will face Mordred without it — and leave no room for doubt about the outcome," Myrddin replied sadly.

Malcolm tugged at his ear. "What about the sword in the stone altar? What will become of it?"

Myrddin shrugged. "I suppose it will stay there until Arthur can come back to retrieve it."

"Yeah, right," Jeff said. "Maybe I'll try to pull it out when we get back."

"Maybe you should," Myrddin agreed.

Malcolm glanced over at the old man. "How do you know all of this? Are you really Merlin or a descendent?"

Myrddin smiled. "I'm simply a vessel of God, here to do his bidding."

Jeff thought on that for a few moments and obviously found it lacking as an answer. "Come on, tell us straight out. Are you Merlin or aren't you?"

Myrddin turned in the front seat to face him, and his eyes sparkled. *"What do you believe?"*

Epilogue

In the year following their adventure with King Arthur, Malcolm and Jeff kept an eye on the news from Britain. The Fordes — Alan, Jane, and Elizabeth — joined them in what became a small group of *Arthurphiles*. They met and discussed the impact of Arthur's visit on the United Kingdom. The impact was significant.

Reports were sensational at first as the nation dealt with the events from Wellsbridge. Christ Church became the center of attention, as expected. Initially, it was a curiosity to those who wanted to see the miraculous sword in the stone altar. Silliness soon followed as Arthur-sightings were claimed all over the world. Then, as often happens, the national and international press turned their fickle attention to other things, leaving room for a more serious phenomenon to take place.

Christ Church became a source of a remarkable spiritual renewal that spread in churches throughout the country. Many said it was based on something more important than the sword or even stories of Arthur's appearance — it was a stronger and deeper movement that stirred "the childlike faith in the hearts of true Christian believers," or so Graham had written to Malcolm.

Graham, who grew from strength to strength to become a leading light in the Church of England, also wrote that it wasn't only a childlike faith, but the actions resulting from that faith. "It's a choice we all have to make," he wrote. "We must know what we believe and then act on it."

Malcolm thought that summed the experience up nicely.

Shamed by the scandal over Christ Church, Ponsonby disappeared from public life. Some reports said he'd beat a hasty retreat to Switzerland, never to return to England. The arch-deacon went into a forced early retirement after rumors persisted that his role in the whole affair was not entirely innocent.

Myrddin lived quietly in his cottage, resisting the attempts of some to turn him into a celebrity prophet.

As for Arthur, he met Mordred on the battlefield just as legend said. Though he knew he would die, he went forward anyway and succeeded in stopping Mordred's reign of terror. He knew what he believed and acted upon it.

As for the sword, it remains in the stone altar even to this day, waiting for the once and future king to draw it out.

memory's gate

paul mccusker

Read chapter 1 of *Memory's Gate*,
Book 3 in the Time Thriller Trilogy.

1

What in the world am I doing here? Elizabeth Forde asked herself
as she followed a silver-haired woman down the main hallway of
the Fawlt Line Retirement Center.

*Of all the things I could have spent the rest of my summer
doing, why this?* Yes, she had agreed to volunteer at the retirement center. She had even felt enthusiastic about the idea at
the time. But walking down the cold, clinical, pale green hallway
which smelled of pine disinfectant, Elizabeth wondered if she had
made a mistake.

She'd been swept along by Reverend Armstrong's passion-
ate call to the young people of the church. He had exuberantly
insisted that they get involved in the community. They must be
a generation of givers rather than takers, he'd said. His words
were powerful and persuasive, and before she knew what she
was doing she had joined a line of other young people to sign up
for volunteer service. Just a few hours a day, three or four days a
week, for a couple of weeks. It hadn't sounded like much.

An old man, bent over like a question-mark, stepped out of his room and smiled toothlessly at her.

It's too much, she thought. *Let me out of here*.

"I know what you're thinking," said her guide, Mrs. Kottler, with a smile. "You're thinking that a few hours a day simply won't be enough. You'll want more time. Everyone feels that way. But if you do the best you can with the hours you have, you'll be just fine. I promise. Maybe later, once you've proven yourself, we'll let you come in longer."

Elizabeth smiled noncommittally.

Mrs. Kottler wore masterfully applied makeup, discreet gold jewelry, and a fashionable dark blue dress. She smelled of expensive perfume. Elizabeth thought she looked more like a real estate agent than the administrator of an old folks' home.

"We don't call it an 'old folks home,' by the way," Mrs. Kottler said, as if she'd read Elizabeth's mind, "or a 'sanitarium' or any of those other outdated names. It's just what the sign says: it's a retirement center. People have productive and active lives here. Being a senior citizen doesn't mean you have one foot in the grave. People who retire at sixty-five often have another twenty or thirty years to enjoy their lives. We're here to help them do it as well as it can be done."

Elizabeth glanced at a couple of productive and active people staring blankly at the television sets in their rooms.

"Of course, we do have *older* residents who have gone beyond their mental or physical capacity to jog around the center six times a day, if you know what I mean," Mrs. Kottler added as they rounded a corner and walked briskly down a short corridor toward two large doors. "For the everyone else, there's a full schedule of activities throughout the day. Most take place here in the recreation room."

Mrs. Kottler pushed on the two doors, which swung open grandly to reveal a large room filled with game tables, easels, a large-screen television, and bookcases filled with hundreds of books and magazines. Unlike the main halls and cafeteria Elizabeth had just seen, this room was decorated warmly with wooden end tables, lace doilies, and the kinds of chairs and sofas found in showcase living rooms. Tastefully painted scenes of sunlit hills, lush green valleys, and golden rivers adorned the walls.

"Pretty, huh? I decorated this one myself," Mrs. Kottler said. "I know what you're thinking. You're thinking that they should have let me decorate the entire center. Well, that wasn't my decision to make. The residents are responsible for decorating their own rooms any way they like. Most of the other assembly areas were done before I joined the staff."

"How long have you been working here?" Elizabeth asked politely.

"Five years," Mrs. Kottler answered. She added wistfully, "Time. It goes by so quickly, don't you find?"

For Elizabeth, who had been only eleven when Mrs. Kottler started her job, the last five years hadn't gone by quickly at all. She had traveled from the carefree days of Barbie dolls to the insecurities of middle school and now to the early stages of womanhood and wide-eyed wonder over her future. And she had also traveled to a parallel time — not that she'd be inclined to mention such a thing to Mrs. Kottler. *No, it hasn't gone by very quickly*, she thought. And as she considered the residents of the center and realized that one day *she* might have to live in a place like this, she hoped life would never go by that quickly. She shuddered at the thought.

As Elizabeth was contemplatimg, a tall, handsome young man entered through a door at the opposite end of the recreation room. "Mrs. K, I was wondering — "

"Doug Hall, come meet Elizabeth Forde," Mrs. Kottler said, waving her arms as if she might create enough of a breeze to sail Doug over to them.

Doug strode across the room with a smile that showed off the deep dimples in his cheeks. *He's a movie star*, Elizabeth thought. His curly brown hair, perfectly formed face, large brown eyes, and a painstakingly sculpted physique that was enhanced, not hidden, by the white clinical coat made her certain. *He's a movie star playing a doctor*, she decided.

Doug outstretched a hand and said, "Well, my enjoyment of this place just increased by a hundred percent."

She shook his hand and blushed. "Hi."

"Doug is our maintenance engineer," Mrs. Kottler explained.

Doug smiled again. "She means I'm the main janitor. But I'm more like a bouncer, in case these old merrymakers get out of control with their wild partying and carousing."

"Stop it, Doug," Mrs. Kottler said with a giggle. Then she turned to Elizabeth. "I know what you're thinking. You're thinking, what's a good-looking and charming young man like him doing in a place like this?"

For once, Mrs. Kottler had it right. *He's a movie star playing a janitor?* It didn't seem appropriate somehow. She waited for the answer.

"Well, if you can find out, please let me know," Mrs. Kottler said with another giggle. "He won't tell anyone. I assume he has a deep, dark secret. Perhaps he was involved in some sort of intrigue in France and barely escaped from the police on his yacht. Why else would he be hiding in a retirement center in a small town?"

"If you have to know the truth, I ran off with the church funds," Doug said. He and Mrs. Kottler chuckled as if this little exchange had been their own private joke for a long time.

Doug rested his gaze on Elizabeth, making her feel self-conscious about how she appeared to him. How did she look in her freshly issued white-and-pink clinic jacket — frumpy or professional? Had she taken enough time with her makeup? Were her large brown eyes properly accented? Did her smile look natural? Her skin was freshly tanned, and she had no unsightly pimples, which made her glad. She'd tied back her long brown hair, but now she wished she had let it fall loose. It looked better that way, Jeff always said.

Jeff.

Thinking of her boyfriend at that moment gave her pause — as if her self-conscious vanity was, in and of itself, an act of infidelity to him. She glanced away from Doug self-consciously.

"Well, back to business," Doug said pleasantly, as if he'd picked up on her feelings and wanted to spare her any embarrassment. "I was wondering if now would be a good time to adjust the settings on the Jacuzzi. You don't have any plans to let the kids in this afternoon, right?"

"No, Doug, the 'kids' won't be going in today," Mrs. Kottler replied. "Do whatever you need to do."

He nodded. "Maybe Elizabeth will want to test it later when I'm finished." He gave her a coy grin.

"I think Elizabeth will be too busy getting acclimated to her new duties," Mrs. Kottler replied.

Doug tipped a finger against his brow as a farewell. "If there's anything I can do to help ..."

Mrs. Kottler watched him go. "He's such a flirt. A charming, good-looking flirt, but a flirt nonetheless." Elizabeth detected a hint of jealousy in her voice.

The tour of the center eventually led Elizabeth and Mrs. Kottler outside to the five acres of manicured grounds, landscaped into gentle green slopes that ultimately rolled down to a small manmade body of water called Richards Lake. It was enclosed on one side by a natural forest that extended off to the horizon. Elizabeth walked alongside Mrs. Kottler, feeling oppressed by the humidity of the August afternoon. She swatted at the occasional mosquito that wanted to make a meal of her arms.

"The heat and mosquitos tend to keep everyone inside on days like this," Mrs. Kottler said.

"Except those two," Elizabeth said, gesturing to two people in a white Victorian-style gazebo near the lake.

"That's Sheriff Hounslow and his father," Mrs. Kottler said with just enough annoyance to betray her usual professional detachment. "I suppose we should say a quick hello."

As they got closer, Elizabeth saw that the sheriff, a large man in a light gray uniform, was pacing in an agitated way. His father, a shadow from this distance, was sitting on one of the benches that lined the gazebo. Sheriff Hounslow saw them coming and waved.

Mrs. Kottler spoke to Elizabeth in a low voice. "Adam Hounslow joined us just a couple of days ago. Like many new residents, he's having a hard time adjusting. Hello, Sheriff!"

Mrs. Kottler and Elizabeth mounted the steps to the shade in the round white roof covering the gazebo. The heat and humidity didn't change.

"Look who's here," Sheriff Hounslow announced. "Mrs. Kottler and — well, well — Elizabeth Forde."

"Oh, you know my new volunteer. Elizabeth will be with us a few hours a day for the next couple of weeks."

"How nice. You be sure to take special care of my father," the sheriff said. "His name is Adam."

Elizabeth could see the old man clearly now. He was bent over from some sort of arthritis and had a pale, wrinkled face with hazel eyes encased in deep, worried frowns — in them, she could see the resemblance between the father and the son. Wisps of thin white hair sprayed out from a spotted crown.

"Wouldn't you like a pretty girl like Elizabeth to help take care of you, Dad?" the sheriff asked.

"I don't need to be taken care of," the old man growled. He tucked his head down against his chest.

Sheriff Hounslow ignored the remark and continued. "I'm surprised to see you here, Elizabeth. Shouldn't you be getting ready for the grand opening of that historical amusement park, or whatever Malcolm calls it?"

"It's not an amusement park," Elizabeth corrected him. "It's called the Historical Village."

"I didn't know you were connected to Malcolm Dubbs!" Mrs. Kottler said, impressed. Malcolm Dubbs was the closest thing Fawlt Line had to royalty, a member of the English branch of the Dubbs family that had been in the area for nearly 300 years. Malcolm came to manage the estate after the last American adult member of the Dubbs family was killed in a car accident.

"She's also dating Jeff Dubbs," the sheriff informed her.

"Are you? Doug will be very disappointed," Mrs. Kottler teased, then said earnestly, "Jeff's parents died in that terrible accident awhile back, didn't they? That was so sad."

Elizabeth nodded without responding. Jeff's parents — Malcolm's cousin and his wife — had died in a plane crash a couple of years before, and so Jeff lived with Malcolm.

Mrs. Kottler fluttered her eyes as if she might cry. "I think Malcolm Dubbs is a remarkable man. Imagine taking in that boy."

"*That boy* is the true heir to the estate," the sheriff interjected sarcastically. "If I were him, I'd have a lot of trouble with Malcolm using the family money to build that park."

"It's not Jeff's money unless Malcolm dies," Elizabeth corrected him. "He's entitled to do whatever he wants with it. And Jeff is very proud of Malcolm."

Mrs. Kottler nodded. "After all, Malcolm is using it to create something everyone will learn from. It's not as if he's wasting it." She turned to Elizabeth. "Is it true that he's brought in authentic buildings, displays, and artifacts from all over the world?"

"Whatever he can find. From picture frames and hairbrushes to school houses and church ruins, as much as he could find from the past few hundred years is represented." She covered a smile, realizing she was reciting one of Malcolm's brochures. "Phase One opens on Saturday."

"Phase One?"

"Malcolm says the village is a work in progress. He'll open various sections of it as they're ready."

"As I said, it's a Disneyland of history," the sheriff said derisively.

Elizabeth frowned at Sheriff Hounslow, knowing better than most the adversarial relationship the two men had. Elizabeth suspected that the sheriff was jealous of Malcolm's wealth and the respect he commanded from the townspeople. But whatever the reason, Hounslow never missed an opportunity to poke fun at Malcolm's projects or eccentricities.

"I can't wait to go on the rides!" he added.

"Are there rides?" Mrs. Kottler asked, amazed.

Elizabeth shook her head. "No. Just buildings and displays."

Sheriff Hounslow grinned. "There's going to be a big celebration. The mayor will be there as well as a special assistant to the governor, and there'll be a telegram from the president and maybe even world peace — all thanks to Malcolm Dubbs."

"Don't be such a pompous fool, Richard," Adam Hounslow barked at his son. "I'm looking forward to seeing the village."

"I'm glad you're looking forward to something," the sheriff remarked.

"Living in a place like this, I'm lucky to look forward to anything," Adam snapped.

"Oh, I'm sure you don't mean that," Mrs. Kottler said. "The Fawlt Line Retirement Center will be like home to you in no time at all, I promise."

Adam scowled at her. "This will never be my home. My home has been sold right out from under me by my thoughtful and compassionate son."

"I'm not getting into this argument with you again, Dad," Hounslow said irritably.

"Yes you will," Adam replied. "As long as you force me to live in places where I don't want to live, we'll have this argument."

The sheriff turned on his father. "Where else are you going to live? You couldn't stay in that big old place alone. You can barely take care of yourself, let alone keep up with a big house."

The old man snorted and turned away.

Sheriff Hounslow wouldn't let it go. "Do I have to remind you of what led up to this? Do I have to announce to the whole world how you nearly burnt the house down — twice — by forgetting to turn the stove burners off? Or the time you flooded the house by wandering off to the store while the bath water was running?"

Mrs. Kottler caught Elizabeth's eyes and jerked her head toward the center, signaling that they should leave. Heading across the grounds, Elizabeth could still hear the voices of the two men arguing behind her.

"I know what you're thinking," Mrs. Kottler said. "You're thinking that Adam must be crazy not to like our center. Well, I agree. But he'll get used to it. They always do."

They approached the building from the back, where a stone patio had been added to the recreation room. It was congested with plants and flowers of all kinds. A man in a wheelchair was pruning the plants, meticulously spraying the leaves with a water bottle and wiping them. He had long gray hair that poured out from under a large baseball cap. Beneath the brim of the cap he wore sunglasses so dark that Elizabeth couldn't see his eyes at all. A bushy mustache and beard flowed downward. It struck her that, apart from his cheeks, his face couldn't be seen at all. He wore a baggy jogging suit that, to Elizabeth's thinking, must have been unbearably hot in the heat and humidity.

"That's Mr. Betterman, another new resident," Mrs. Kottler said. "Come meet him."

They crossed the patio and Mrs. Kottler introduced them.

Mr. Betterman didn't speak, but grunted and held a carnation out to her.

"Very nice," Elizabeth said.

"Take it," Mrs. Kottler whispered.

Elizabeth reached out to take the flower. For a second he didn't let go, but used the moment to lean closer to her and whisper, "I know who you are." He gave her a slight smile then turned away to fiddle with the planter.

Disconcerted, Elizabeth looked to Mrs. Kottler again, who gently shrugged. They walked inside.

"What did he mean by that?" Mrs. Kottler asked once they were inside and clear of Betterman's hearing.

"I don't know," Elizabeth replied. She didn't say, but something about the man's half-smile and voice seemed familiar to her.

"Still, that's quite an honor," Mrs. Kottler said. "He doesn't usually talk to anyone. He's a little eccentric."

No kidding, Elizabeth thought.

As they drifted through the recreation room, Elizabeth found herself looking for Doug. She wasn't a flirtatious person — nor was she interested in anyone but Jeff — and yet she was drawn to him. Maybe because he was someone else in the building who was young and sympathetic, like her.

Mrs. Kottler smiled contentedly. "Well, that's most of it. I know what you're thinking. You're thinking that this is more like a beautiful hotel than a retirement center. We do our best. Now, let me show you where the storage closets are and introduce you to your new responsibilities."

Forbidden Doors

A Four-Volume Series from Bestselling Author Bill Myers!

Some doors are better left unopened.

Join teenager Rebecca "Becka" Williams, her brother Scott, and her friend Ryan Riordan as they head for mind-bending clashes between the forces of darkness and the kingdom of God.

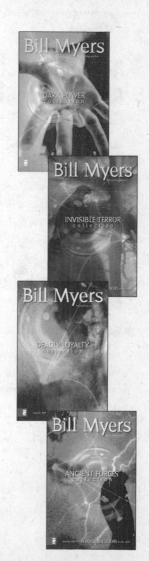

Dark Power Collection
Volume One

Softcover • ISBN: 978-0-310-71534-4

Contains books 1–3: *The Society, The Deceived,* and *The Spell*

Invisible Terror Collection
Volume Two

Softcover • ISBN: 978-0-310-71535-1

Contains books 4–6: *The Haunting, The Guardian,* and *The Encounter*

Deadly Loyalty Collection
Volume Three

Softcover • ISBN: 978-0-310-71536-8

Contains books 7–9: *The Curse, The Undead,* and *The Scream*

Ancient Forces Collection
Volume Four

Softcover • ISBN: 978-0-310-71537-5

Contains books 10–12: *The Ancients, The Wiccan,* and *The Cards*

Echoes from the Edge

A New Trilogy from Bestselling Author Bryan Davis!

This fast-paced adventure fantasy trilogy starts with murder and leads teenagers Nathan and Kelly out of their once-familiar world as they struggle to find answers to the tragedy. A mysterious mirror with phantom images, a camera that takes pictures of things they can't see, and a violin that unlocks unrecognizable voices ... each enigma takes the teens farther into an alternate universe where nothing is as it seems.

Beyond the Reflection's Edge
Book One

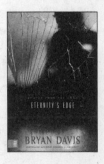

Softcover • ISBN: 978-0-310-71554-2

After sixteen-year-old Nathan Shepherd's parents are murdered during a corporate investigation, he teams up with a friend to solve the case. They discover mirrors that reflect events from the past and future, a camera that photographs people who aren't there, and a violin that echoes unseen voices.

Eternity's Edge
Book Two

Softcover • ISBN: 978-0-310-71555-9

Nathan Shepherd's parents are alive after all! With the imminent collapse of the universe at hand, due to a state called interfinity, Nathan sets out to find them. With Kelly at his side, he must balance his efforts between searching for his parents and saving the world. Will Nathan be reunited with his parents?

Book 3 coming soon!

Pick up a copy today at your favorite bookstore!

Visit www.zondervan.com/teen

Share Your Thoughts

With the Author: Your comments will be forwarded to
the author when you send them to *zauthor@zondervan.com*.

With Zondervan: Submit your review of this book
by writing to *zreview@zondervan.com*.

Free Online Resources at
www.zondervan.com/hello

 Zondervan AuthorTracker: Be notified whenever your
favorite authors publish new books, go on tour, or post
an update about what's happening in their lives.

 Daily Bible Verses and Devotions: Enrich your life
with daily Bible verses or devotions that help you start
every morning focused on God.

 Free Email Publications: Sign up for newsletters on
fiction, Christian living, church ministry, parenting, and
more.

 Zondervan Bible Search: Find and compare
Bible passages in a variety of translations at
www.zondervanbiblesearch.com.

 Other Benefits: Register yourself to receive online
benefits like coupons and special offers, or to participate
in research.